A Montana Christmas

2 Stories in 1!

The Stone brothers are about to celebrate
Christmas in two very surprising ways!

Rancher Jared Stone has taken in gorgeous single
mom Melanie Briggs and her baby. Meanwhile,
Will Stone is stranded out of town in a blizzard
with Melanie's sassy, stylish cousin,
Ms. Dylan Briggs.

Two sexy bachelors.

Two feisty women.

One very special Temptation volume.

Enjoy!

USA TODAY *bestselling author Kristine Rolofson
is one of North America's best-loved writers*

Dear Reader,

Do you remember your first Christmas away from home? I was a nineteen-year-old bride of three months, celebrating the holidays in a farmhouse in Nebraska with my in-laws. It was a long way from the East Coast! I'd always wanted to be part of a large family and there I was, surrounded by Rolofsons. There were so many of them that they hired a hall in order to have a potluck Christmas dinner.

When I told my new husband that I didn't feel well, that I couldn't eat, I wanted to cry and my stomach felt tied up in knots, he told me I was homesick. Homesick? It was a new and awful feeling, eased by the kindness of my new family, but never completely gone until I boarded the plane to go home. *Home*. What a wonderful word!

A Montana Christmas is all about spending the holidays with someone you love. Whether you are the one going home—or the person cleaning it for those much-loved guests—I hope you spend your Christmas enjoying every moment with the people who mean the most to you. And give that new daughter-in-law an extra hug from me.

Merry Christmas!

Kristine Rolofson

Books by Kristine Rolofson

HARLEQUIN TEMPTATION
842—A WIFE FOR OWEN CHASE
850—A BRIDE FOR CALDER BROWN
858—A MAN FOR MAGGIE MOORE
877—THE BABY AND THE BACHELOR

Kristine Rolofson
A Montana Christmas

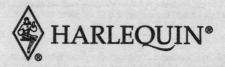

HARLEQUIN®

TORONTO • NEW YORK • LONDON
AMSTERDAM • PARIS • SYDNEY • HAMBURG
STOCKHOLM • ATHENS • TOKYO • MILAN • MADRID
PRAGUE • WARSAW • BUDAPEST • AUCKLAND

If you purchased this book without a cover you should be aware
that this book is stolen property. It was reported as "unsold and
destroyed" to the publisher, and neither the author nor the
publisher has received any payment for this "stripped book."

To Marje, George, Phyllis and Nancy,
the Rolofson siblings who have always
made me feel part of the family.

ISBN 0-373-69106-8

A MONTANA CHRISTMAS

Copyright © 2002 by Kristine Rolofson.

All rights reserved. Except for use in any review, the reproduction or
utilization of this work in whole or in part in any form by any electronic,
mechanical or other means, now known or hereafter invented, including
xerography, photocopying and recording, or in any information storage
or retrieval system, is forbidden without the written permission of the
publisher, Harlequin Enterprises Limited, 225 Duncan Mill Road,
Don Mills, Ontario, Canada M3B 3K9.

All characters in this book have no existence outside the imagination of
the author and have no relation whatsoever to anyone bearing the same
name or names. They are not even distantly inspired by any individual
known or unknown to the author, and all incidents are pure invention.

This edition published by arrangement with Harlequin Books S.A.

® and TM are trademarks of the publisher. Trademarks indicated with
® are registered in the United States Patent and Trademark Office, the
Canadian Trade Marks Office and in other countries.

Visit us at www.eHarlequin.com

Printed in U.S.A.

WHAT CHILD IS THIS?

1

Monday, December 16
Havre, Montana

TAKE GOOD CARE OF HER.

Those were Will's words on the phone. Well, of course he would do as Will asked. That's what a brother did, and Jared Stone took his family duties seriously. Maybe a little too seriously, some would say. But there was nothing wrong with that, Jared figured, working his way through the crowd in a train station filled with holiday travelers and the people who waited to greet them. A man took care of his own.

Jared saw a lot of people with shopping bags filled with gifts, tired mothers holding on to toddlers, grandmothers kissing squalling babies and a few businessmen trying to avoid walking into groups of families huddled together to say hello or goodbye.

There were skiers, too. There were always skiers heading somewhere in Montana. Jared took a second to admire a long-legged blonde carrying skis and wearing tight black leggings and a sheepskin jacket, but he kept moving through the crowd as he headed toward the board that would list the arrival times of

the trains. Sure enough, the train named the Empire
Builder from Chicago had just arrived.

Her name is Melanie Briggs. And she's special. Jared
wished he'd asked Will for more details, but Aunt
Bitty picked up the phone and started talking about
cookies and presents and how much Fluffy liked
spending Christmas on the ranch. Will wasn't able to
add much about his mysterious guest, but everyone
at the ranch assumed that Will had finally found a
woman. A special woman. He'd said so himself,
hadn't he?

The 318 on Monday. As Jared looked around the
lobby he wished his younger brother had provided a
better description of his guest. There had been something about a red jacket, but then Mom had taken the
receiver from Bitty and asked Will if he preferred
sage green or sea foam on the guest-room walls. Then
Uncle Joe got on the kitchen extension and asked if
the future houseguest played bridge.

I'll fill you in when I see you. Then Will's cell phone
broke up and the connection was lost seconds later.
Jared would have asked why the woman was making
a three-day train trip instead of flying to Great Falls,
which was what Will would do tomorrow to get
home for Christmas.

He also would have asked how Will met her. And
why he'd invited her to spend Christmas at the ranch,
but Will was famous for inviting people to visit Graystone. His brother, always the adventurer, collected
friends wherever he traveled. But he'd never invited

one lone woman—one designated for special treatment—home until now.

So the next afternoon, after trying three times to call his brother and getting only Will's voice mail, Jared drove the hundred and sixty miles north to Havre, a good-size town just south of the Canadian border, to meet a stranger. A stranger his younger brother called "special." He'd practically had to hogtie his mother to the kitchen table to keep her from making the trip, but he'd needed to take the truck and he didn't think either woman would be comfortable riding for three hours in the back section of the king cab.

"I'll have dinner ready then," Jenna Stone declared, with a sideways glance at Aunt Bitty, who was busy plugging her radio into a receptacle above the counter. "I wouldn't have minded getting out of the house for a while, though."

"No," he'd said, figuring the next suggestion would be for Jenn to meet the train by herself, and with the way the sky looked, they were in for snow. And a lot of it. They might need the four-wheel-drive truck, and his mother's Explorer was in the shop getting new brakes and wouldn't be ready until tomorrow.

Jared continued searching through the crowds and looking for a special-looking woman who might or might not be wearing a red coat. He should have brought one of those signs chauffeurs hold, and the thought made him smile.

He skirted the edge of the crowd and looked for

someone who appeared to be waiting for a ride. A middle-aged woman with two small children sat on a bench, her suitcases piled around her. And a couple of college-age girls, expectant expressions on their pretty faces, stood on tiptoe and peered over the crowd. He caught a glimpse of a cherry-red coat and dark hair curling to a woman's shoulders and hurried toward her. If she would only turn around, he thought, he could say something like, "Are you waiting for Jared Stone?"

She turned toward him, almost as if hearing his unspoken plea, and revealed pale skin, large eyes and a heart-shaped face that was nothing short of perfect. Her red coat, age and the expression on her face, as if she was waiting for help, made Jared feel as if he'd hit pay dirt.

She was lovely, a fragile-looking young woman who obviously needed rescuing. Her eyes widened when she spotted him a few feet away from her. Jared knew no one could deny the Stone family resemblance. He and Will both looked like their father, though Will was leaner. Jared smiled, but was stalled on his way to greet her as two elderly women shoved suitcases in his path and waved gloved hands toward the exit. Jared reached down to help them, earning the fluttering thanks of the Bailey sisters, old friends of his grandparents who had moved to Havre a few years back.

"You look just like your grandfather," one of them announced. "I'd know that Stone chin anywhere."

"Are you looking for someone?" Jared asked. In

other words, was there someone who could assist the Baileys so he'd be free to collect his guest and begin the drive home?

"Mr. Perkins is over there," the other sister, the shorter one, said. "He's come to collect us, but I don't think he's seen us yet. My, what a crowd this afternoon. It certainly is festive."

Jared didn't know who Mr. Perkins was, but he obligingly turned to look where the elder Miss Bailey pointed. He caught the eye of the station's porter and waved him over to help.

"The porter's coming to carry these suitcases for you," Jared reassured the women. "Just stay where you are."

"Thank you, dear," the taller Miss Bailey beamed. "Please wish your dear mother a merry Christmas for us."

"Yes, ma'am," he said, tipping the brim of his Stetson before turning back to the dark-haired beauty in the red coat. She was no longer there, which gave him a jolt of unfamiliar panic. Jared Stone wasn't a man to panic easily, if ever, but he sure as hell didn't want to lose his brother's special guest.

Jared pushed through the thinning crowd and saw the red-coated young woman seated, bundles of blankets on her lap, on a bench along the wall between the rest rooms. Her head was tilted back against the wall, almost as if she'd resigned herself to resting there for a long, long time. She clutched the bundle in her arms as if it was her only and most sacred possession.

This time he made sure he said her name. "Mela-

nie?'' She didn't move, so this time he said it much
louder.

"*Melanie,*" he called, surprising himself with how
loud he'd said the word, but satisfied when her head
lifted and she met his gaze. He willed himself to
smile, though he felt as if a bolt of summer lightning
had hit him right in the middle of the train station.

She was beautiful, he realized again, when her lips
lifted into a smile of greeting. He moved around a
chubby grandfather, who bent over a little boy to
make sure his jacket was zipped shut, to approach
her. Finally.

"You *are* Melanie Briggs, I hope," he said, stepping
close enough to see that her eyes were lined in dark
shadows and she looked like she could use some rest.
Two and a half days on a train couldn't be much fun.

"Yes. Jared Stone?"

"Yeah."

"I'm so glad to see you."

"Same here." He wished he'd thought to bring pillows; the woman looked tired enough to sleep all the
way back to the ranch.

"I saw you a moment ago," she said, her voice low
and soft. "And then you stopped to greet the older
ladies and I thought I had been mistaken after all."

"I look too much like my brother to fool anyone,"
Jared said, wondering why he wanted to scoop her
into his arms and carry her out the door. Only because she looked as if she'd fall over if she stood, he
assured himself. Not for any other reason than that.

"Will told me I would know you when I saw you, but I didn't really believe him."

"Come on." He reached for the large suitcase at her feet. "Let's get out of here."

"I'd like that," she said, adjusting the bundle in her arms. That's when he looked down and saw the pink face of a sleeping baby. That's when his heart stopped beating for a second or two, long enough to scare him, as he stared down at the baby in his house-guest's arms.

"Will didn't tell you I had a daughter?"

"No." Jared looked up. The woman gripped the baby, wrapped securely in what looked like a mountain of blankets, with a fierce protectiveness. "It was a bad connection."

"He told me it would be okay, that no one would mind."

"No one will," he said, silently cursing his brother for not warning them. Melanie stood, managing to sling a purse and an oversize quilted bag over her shoulder at the same time. The baby never made a sound, though Jared caught a glimpse of its eyes as they popped open to stare up at Melanie.

"The car seat is mine, too," she said, so Jared picked it up. It wasn't Will's child, of course, he assured himself as he motioned the woman toward the exit. There was no way his brother could have kept such a secret from the family for such a long time. Besides, if the child was Will's, she would have had the Stone name and live at Graystone ranch by now.

"The suitcase rolls," Melanie said. "You can pull out the handle and—"

"This is faster," Jared countered, holding the black case by its handle, along with the plastic seat contraption. The crowd had thinned now, and there was no sign of the Bailey sisters. "Go on toward the door. I'm right behind you."

He stayed close enough to touch that dark hair with his fingers, not that he did so. This one was special, Will had said. This woman was Will's and was, therefore, to be protected at all costs. Even if she was a stranger who carried an infant.

Their mother was going to be beside herself with joy. She'd longed for grandchildren for years, since her sons had been old enough to get married and bring brides to the ranch. There had been no brides, not until now. The Stone sons showed little inclination to settle down.

Melanie paused at the door and rearranged the blankets around the baby's face while Jared reached out and pushed the door open for her. The cold wind hit them with cruel force, and Melanie hunched over the child and didn't seem to notice that Jared's arm lay across her shoulder to guide her to the parking lot. When they rounded the corner of the building, the wind eased and he dropped his hand from her back.

"So this is Havre," she said, looking across the railroad yard to a restaurant famous for serving food quickly to train passengers who would continue west

after a short stop in northern Montana. She pro-
nounced the word "Hay-ver."

"Have-er," Jared said, raising his voice to be heard
above the wind. They waited for a line of cars to pass
before they could cross the street. "It was supposed to
be named for a French town, but local legend has a
different version."

She looked at him and prompted, "Which is?"

"Two fur trappers were fighting over a woman,
and one of them decided he wasn't going to get killed
deciding who won, so he said, 'You can have-er.'"

"Have her," she repeated, and the briefest of smiles
flashed across her face. "You're not teasing? This is a
true story?"

"I don't know about true, but it's on a sign here at
the train station," he declared. "You want to see it?"

She shivered. "Not today."

"Then come on," Jared said, urging her across the
street by touching her back once again. She felt small
and delicate, as if the north wind would pick her up
and blow her to Wyoming if she wasn't weighted
down by a blanket-wrapped child. What was Will
thinking by inviting this woman and her baby to
Graystone? His brother would have a lot of questions
to answer.

ANYONE WOULD KNOW THEY were brothers without
having to ask, Melanie decided. Will and his older
brother shared the same broad shoulders and dark
hair, identical stubborn chins and skin color. Will's
eyes were brown, not Jared's unusual shade of dark

green. His face was narrower, his expression more relaxed, but their hair waved in similar patterns across their foreheads and both brothers walked as if they knew exactly where they were going, all of the time.

She would have enjoyed the walk to Jared Stone's truck if she hadn't been worried about Beth feeling the fierce wind that pushed at them from behind. Melanie didn't mind the wind that much. Fresh air had been in short supply on the train. She noticed that Will's brother adjusted his long strides so she could keep up with him, even though she was already walking as fast as she could without breaking into a jog.

He settled her and Beth into the passenger seat of an oversize truck, then went around to the driver's side and proceeded to figure out how to install the baby's car seat into the back section of the truck. "It's a long ride" was all the man said. "Do you want to put, ah, her in the seat before we get started?"

"Yes. Thanks."

He was around to her side of the truck almost instantly and helped her get down. She felt awkward and old and close to tears by the time she settled Beth into the seat, the straps adjusted over her tiny body. Luckily her daughter liked to ride and would sleep for a while. A long while, Melanie hoped. Jared Stone hadn't been expecting a baby and wasn't prepared for Beth's fussing.

"All set?" His voice was a low rumble behind her, reminding Melanie that she needed to climb back into the truck once again. She needed to stop fretting, too.

"Yes," she assured him. Things will work out, Will had promised Saturday afternoon when he helped her onto the train. *Quit worrying.* "Everything's fine."

"I guess you've never been to Montana before?" His question was polite, but his attention was on starting the truck and checking the rearview mirror before he backed out of the parking space.

"No. Will warned me that it would be cold." And private, too. She rubbed the condensation from the side window and saw some of Havre before Jared drove the truck onto a main road. And then there wasn't much to see except snow-coated grasslands and an occasional house. She unfastened her seat belt so she could check to see that Beth was breathing. Sure enough, the baby slept without a care in the world, her cheeks pink and her little lips pursed as if she dreamt of being fed.

"What else did he tell you?"

"He said your mother likes Christmas." *He said that I would be able to hide. And heal. And pretend that the huge black hole that was now my life would be invisible.*

He chuckled. "*Likes* Christmas? That's an understatement. Our mother is Santa Claus, Martha Stewart and Bing Crosby rolled into one."

"Why Bing Crosby?"

"She sings along to his Christmas CDs while she cooks. Right now she's decorating the guest room for you."

"I hope she's not going to any trouble." She had made Will promise that her visit wouldn't inconvenience his family.

"Don't worry. She's been having a great time since we got a satellite dish. Mom discovered the decorating and design channels and has been fixing up the house ever since."

She heard laughter in his voice, and affection. "I'm sorry Will didn't tell any of you that I was bringing a baby. I just assumed he'd said something before he invited us."

"My mother is used to surprises from Will." He turned on the defroster, then stepped on the gas pedal to pass a large van. Melanie looked out the window and rested her head against the back of the seat. It would be so easy to close her eyes and be lulled to sleep. In an attempt to be polite, she tried to stay awake. The oncoming cars had their headlights on now that the sky had grown darker. She looked at her watch. Four o'clock. More than twenty-four hours since she and Beth had boarded the train at Union Station. Her cousin Dylan would be having a fit, but she would have to understand that a Christmas with the family wasn't something she was ready for. Not yet.

"We're going to be on the road for about two and a half hours," Jared said, breaking the silence. "Maybe more, because I think we'll stay on the main highway and then pick up Highway 200 at Great Falls."

"All right." She had no idea what he was talking about.

"We'll stop there for coffee and, uh, anything else you need for the baby." He glanced toward Melanie and surprised her with the serious expression on his face. "Do you think she's okay back there?"

"She's sleeping," she assured him. "She likes to ride."

"Good thing," he murmured. "See that sky? We're going to get some more snow, and soon."

Melanie looked out the window and craned her neck upward to see dark gray clouds and approaching darkness. "We won't get stuck, will we?"

"No. We'll be home in time for a late supper. Unless you want to stop and get something on the road. I should have asked if you were hungry."

"I'm fine," she said, though it had been hours since breakfast. Beth had been fussy most of the afternoon and there had been no time to eat the sandwich another traveler had purchased for her in the dining car.

"If you change your mind, just say so." He switched on the radio and a woman with a country twang sang about love in the afternoon. Jared hurried to turn it off. "Sorry," he said. "I forgot about waking the baby. What's her name?"

"Beth. And the music won't bother her." At least the song had filled the truck and substituted for conversation.

She didn't mind the silence.

JENNA LOOKED AT HER WATCH, then at the clock on the wall above the refrigerator. Jared should have their guest by now. They should be on their way home, but she'd been switching back and forth between the Carol Duvall show and the Weather Channel and now she was worried. She'd no interest in rubber-stamping faux wallpaper when another storm was predicted and neither son was home safe and sound.

"They'll be fine. No one's more dependable than Jared," Uncle Joe declared, reading her mind as he entered the large kitchen and poured himself a cup of coffee. He paused before putting the carafe back into place. "You want some, honey?"

"No, thanks. I've got enough jitters as it is." But she gave the old man a smile she hoped was reassuring. He was the last remaining member of her side of the family and, at eighty-two, Uncle Joe was proud of his longevity and his skill with cards. He'd arrived the week before Thanksgiving and, declaring he was lonesome, moved into the enormous ranch house "until the New Year," he'd declared. "Or until you kick me out." He knew Jenna would never do such a thing, but it was a little joke between them. Uncle Joe liked his little jokes.

"You've got no reason to be nervous, honey. Christmas around here is always one hell of an occasion, thanks to you." Uncle Joe pulled out a chair and sat down at the long worktable that had been at the ranch for four generations. "And Will was only in Washington for six weeks. He couldn't get serious about no young woman, not that fast."

"I don't know about that." She would fix a cup of herbal tea, Jenna decided. "My sons have big hearts, though Jared tries to hide it more than Will. And I sure wouldn't mind having a daughter-in-law. I'd about given up hope of ever having another woman for company around here."

"Bitty doesn't count?" The old man shot her an evil grin.

"Aunt Bitty's in a class by herself."

"Where is the old bat, anyway?"

"Uncle Joe—" she began, ready to admonish him again to be nice to her husband's aunt.

"I know, I know." He held up a gnarled hand as if to ward off her words. "She's an in-law and you can't do anything about her. I don't mind her radio shows, but that barking rat of hers is too much for a man to ignore."

Jenna couldn't help her smile. The "barking rat" was Bitty's ancient Maltese, a nine-pound dog who was never out of his devoted owner's sight. Fluffy did everything but eat his meals at the dinner table, and Jenna had no doubt that if she allowed it, that's exactly where he would perch. "Fluffy doesn't bark that much."

"He isn't 'fluffy,' either," Joe grumbled.

"I'm sure his thyroid medication will kick in one of these days." She looked again at the clock and wished she'd told Jared to call her when he left Havre. Her eldest didn't think much of cell phones; he grudgingly kept one in his truck's glove compartment, but rarely used it.

"You spoil us all, Jenn," he declared, taking another sip of coffee. "Like you'll spoil Will's girl, once she gets here. You get that painting done?"

"Yesterday." She hoped Melanie Briggs liked lilac.

"And dinner smells good."

"Yes," she said, taking the kettle off the stove. "I cooked a roast earlier, so no matter what time they arrive dinner will be ready."

"You think of everything," the old man declared, beaming at her. He plucked a deck of cards from his shirt pocket. "You want to play a hand of gin rummy, just to make the time pass quick?"

"Sure." Between Joe's cards, Bitty's radio programs and Fluffy's constant begging for treats, Jenna hoped she wouldn't have time to worry about her sons.

2

SO WHAT IF SHE WAS ONE of the most beautiful women he had ever seen? Oh, there had been some rodeo queens in his past, and that one summer seven years ago when he'd dated the first runner-up for Miss Montana. But there was something about Melanie, a softness that urged him closer though he knew he should stay well away. After all, she had been invited to the ranch by his brother, who was probably head over heels in love with the woman.

And she had a small child, which meant there was an ex-lover or ex-husband somewhere in the picture to complicate things. There was a lot more to Melanie Briggs than met the eye and Jared hoped his little brother knew what he was getting himself into.

He glanced over and saw that her eyes were closed. He knew if he started a conversation she would sit up and attempt to take part, just to be polite. There would be plenty of time to ask questions tomorrow, but he wouldn't be asking them of his houseguest, that was for damn sure. Will's plane was due in at 5:38 and there would be plenty of time on the drive home to find out what was going on.

Another thirty or so miles passed before he woke her.

"Do you want some coffee or tea or something?" Jared slowed the truck and took the exit that led to a large café. Its lights looked welcoming in the dark and a number of semis and pickups filled the parking lot. Snow swirled around in the wind and hit the windshield, but it was nothing serious. Just flurries so far, but they had another hour or so to go before they were home.

"If you're getting some," Melanie said, but she sounded pleased that they were stopping. The baby let out a couple of noisy complaints after hearing her mother's voice.

"Do you want to come in or wait here while I get it?" He pulled the truck into the lot and found a space near the side entrance.

"I'll come with you. Beth's starting to fuss." She unbuckled her seat belt and leaned over the seat to check the child. Sure enough, the baby wailed again as if she wanted something.

"What do you do for that?"

"Change her, feed her, talk to her."

She made it sound simple, but Jared had a good idea that keeping a baby happy wasn't so easy. He'd nursed enough calves and foals back to health to know that babies of any species were demanding creatures.

Before he could offer help, Melanie opened the

door and hopped out, then fiddled with the lever to move the seat forward so she could climb in back with the baby. A blast of cold air burst into the truck, but Jared got out and made sure both doors were shut so the baby wouldn't catch cold.

"Holler when you're done," he told her, and stood by the door, his back to the wind, and waited for Melanie to finish wrapping up the child. Jared shivered but didn't bother to zip his down jacket. Babies and winter didn't go together. Cows at least waited until spring to drop their calves, even though "spring" in Montana was a loose interpretation of the season.

He turned when he heard the woman fumble at the door, and he found himself taking the baby from her so she could climb down unimpeded. The child's face was covered with a pink fuzzy blanket and once again she was wrapped up in a thick bundle. "Are you sure she can breathe in there?"

"I need to keep the wind out of her face." Melanie reached for her child, but Jared—who had a good grip on the kid—hurried toward the door of the restaurant. He was in no mood to stand outside a second more than necessary, and besides, he didn't want to drop the baby while handing her over to her mother.

"Breakfast 24 Hours" read a blinking neon sign beside the door, which made Jared think of pancakes and eggs and an extra side order of bacon. He pushed open the glass door and they were soon inside the stuffy warmth of a large bright room filled with orange booths, metal chairs and Formica-topped tables. A row of black stools lined the counter and a tired-looking waitress said, "Sit anywhere you like, folks."

He turned to Melanie, who reached out to take the flap of blanket away from the baby's face. The baby's blue eyes stared up at him as if she'd never seen a rancher before. Then she screwed up her face and let out a scream of dismay that caused a couple of truckers to look up from their steak and eggs.

"Here, give her to me," Melanie said, and this time Jared was happy to do just that. "Don't take it personally. She doesn't like being wet."

"Oh." He watched as Melanie unwrapped the wad of blankets with gentle hands, then cooed at the little girl.

"You'll feel much better in a minute, sweetheart, I promise."

"I'll get a booth," Jared said, backing up a step.

"Can you take these? I'll be right back." She handed Jared the blankets and put the screaming child against her shoulder. She headed toward the ladies' room, leaving Jared standing at the edge of the room while three older men at a nearby table gave him pitying looks. He shrugged, tossed the blankets over his shoulder and headed toward a corner booth.

"Coffee?" The waitress was right behind him with a half-full carafe.

"Please." He slid into the booth and dumped the blankets next to him against the wall.

"What about your wife?"

"She's not—never mind. You can pour her some, too."

"Just wave when you want me to take your order," she said, after filling the second mug. She pulled a handful of plastic cream containers from her apron pocket and set them on the table.

"Thanks." He took a sip of coffee and thought about having a piece of pie to go along with it. He was starving and there was still another hour and a half to go before they arrived at the ranch. But he'd wait for Melanie, he decided. Once she joined him at the booth and they were facing each other, maybe he could find out what was going on between her and Will.

He'd finished two-thirds of his coffee before she appeared. Her red jacket was over her arm, the baby against her shoulder, the diaper bag banging her hip as she walked. He saw she wore a brown turtleneck a shade darker than her hair and slim blue jeans that belied the fact she'd had a baby a few months ago. A lock of her hair was damp, as if she'd splashed water on her face. She wore no makeup, and didn't need any. Not in his opinion, anyway. She managed to ease into the booth while holding the child against her.

"I'm sorry I took so long," she said, moving the straps of her purse and diaper bag from her shoulder.

"That's your coffee," he said. "If you want tea instead I'll have—".

"Coffee's fine. Thanks." The baby fussed, pulling its little feet up against Melanie's breasts. She moved the child to the crook of her arm. The baby's face was red, its mouth turned down as she looked up at her mother.

"Can I have one of those blankets?" Her cheeks grew pink. "There wasn't room to feed her in the washroom. I hope you're not the type to go running out into the parking lot."

Jared handed over the pink fluffy blanket. He had no idea what she was talking about, not until she draped the blanket carefully around the baby, covering most of the child and, he assumed, her own left breast. No, he wasn't going to run out into the night, but he sure as hell didn't know where he was supposed to look while this woman breast-fed her child. The baby's smacking noises didn't help ease his embarrassment level, either. Melanie, obviously right-handed, took a careful sip of her coffee.

"I can sit at the counter and give you some privacy," he offered, figuring he was the "type," as she put it, to take the easy way out.

"If you'd be more comfortable," she said, her voice soft. "But it doesn't bother me—or Beth. I'm really sorry you have to go through all of this. You don't know me and yet here we are, and there *you* are, and you weren't expecting any of this, only to pick up your brother's friend at the train station."

It was the most he'd heard her say since they'd met. He kept his gaze fixed firmly above her neck, not that there was anything to see. Melanie had lifted her sweater and engineered the blanket so that no one farther away than arm's length would know what was going on. He prayed the covering would stay in place, that the baby wouldn't get rowdy, that nothing would...drip. "Do you want anything to eat?" was all he could manage to say.

"Are you having anything?"

"Yes. You can't beat the pie here." He handed her one of the thick plastic-coated menus propped against a ketchup bottle and watched as her face lit up. She was hungry, he realized, noting that she managed to hold the menu with one hand. "We've got at least an hour and a half before we get home," he added.

She set the menu on the table and smiled. "I would love a chocolate milkshake, some toast and a large glass of ice water."

He turned to catch the waitress's attention and, when she came to their booth, gave the order. She showed no sign of noticing that Melanie was feeding her child, so maybe this wasn't such a strange occurrence after all.

"Will said you have a large cattle ranch."

"We've been lucky." He drained his coffee and

hoped the waitress would return to give him a refill. "The place has been in the family for a long, long time. Where are you from?"

"Massachusetts, originally. And then I lived in D.C."

He waited for her to add something about her family or her reasons for living in Washington, but she took another sip of her coffee and then lifted the edge of the blanket to check on her daughter's progress.

"Why'd you take the train?" he couldn't help asking.

"I'm afraid to fly."

There was more to it, he was sure. *Where's the child's father* was something else he'd like to know. And why the SOB would let his family spend two and a half days on a train to spend the holidays with strangers.

She looked toward the counter as two more men, their hats and coats dusted with snow, entered the restaurant and wiped their boots on the rubber mat near the door. "It's snowing harder now. Will we be all right?"

"It might take us longer to get home, but it would take a lot more snow than this to cause trouble." Jared glanced at the window, but a row of checked curtains hid his view of the parking lot. "This is typical Montana weather, nothing to worry about."

She smiled, a flash of sweetness that threatened his breathing. "Will talked about you a lot. He said, 'Nothing ever bothers my older brother.'"

Well, Will hadn't seen him drink coffee with a breast-feeding woman.

"WE'RE HERE," A GRUFF MALE voice announced. Melanie didn't want to open her eyes. She didn't want to move, either. Not that she could remember where she was, exactly, but this place was warm and quiet, and sleep was such a rare pleasure she couldn't bear for it to end.

"Melanie," the voice repeated. "We're at the ranch."

The ranch. It took several seconds for those words to make sense, but Melanie blinked and opened her eyes as cold air brushed across her face. The tall rancher shut his door with a quiet click, but the overhead light stayed on. Melanie sat up and unbuckled her seat belt. Her neck was stiff, but she'd been in such a deep sleep she didn't mind. She climbed into the back seat as Jared opened the passenger door.

"Be careful getting out. It's snowing pretty hard and it's slippery," he said, but he didn't look the least bit cold as he stood there in the dark. There were snowflakes coating his hair and the shoulders of his bulky jacket. Every inch the western hero, there was something about Jared that radiated strength and calm, a man sure of himself and what mattered in his life. His brother had that same confidence, but with easier manners and a knack for conversation.

She realized she was staring and turned her attention back to unhitching the straps of the car seat and gathering the blankets around her sleeping child. Her arms were so tired that they trembled as she lifted the baby.

"Give her to me," he said. "It's safer that way."

"All right." She covered Beth's face with the corner of the blanket. Behind Jared light glowed, and when he moved the bucket seat forward to take the baby, Melanie saw a large porch and the bright windows of a very big house. She followed him, though not as quickly as she would have liked. The wind blew the breath back into her mouth when she stepped onto the ground, forcing her to lower her head and hurry after Jared as best she could. She slammed the truck's door and hurried through the snow toward a porch so long it appeared to stretch across the entire length of the house and then some. A door opened and she heard a woman's voice call out, but Melanie concentrated on negotiating the three wide steps to the porch before she looked up.

"Oh, thank goodness you're home," a lovely silver-haired woman she assumed was Jared's mother said. "I was so—Jared, is that a *baby*?"

"Yeah. Here." Jared handed Beth to the woman and then his gloved hand tugged Melanie to the opened door and hauled her inside an enormous brown-and-white kitchen that smelled of freshly baked bread and roasting beef. When she would have stopped to wipe her feet on a mat that read Howdy,

Stranger, Jared urged her forward so he could shut the door. He then helped her remove her coat and then, shrugging off his own, hung them both on nearby hooks on a wood-paneled wall.

Jared's mother, Beth snug in her arms, uncovered the baby's face before lifting her green-eyed gaze to her guest. "And you must be Melanie. I'm Jenna Stone, which I'm sure you've guessed already."

"Yes," she began, surprised that Will's mother looked so young. Her silver hair was caught up at her neck with a barrette; she wore black jeans and an oversize black velvet blouse. Her small wrists were encased in silver bracelets, and beaded silver hoops dangled from her ears. "Thank you for inviting me— us. I'm sorry that Will didn't tell you ahead of time that I was bringing my daughter with me."

"Please don't feel that way," the woman said, her voice soft. "We're so glad to meet you. *Both* of you. It's been a long time since we've had a baby in the house." She gazed down at Beth and then back to Melanie. She looked as if she'd been given the best Christmas gift of her life. "Does this mean I'm finally a grandmother?"

"I wouldn't know," was all she could think to say. Jenna looked so disappointed that Melanie almost felt as if she should apologize again. "Will and I—"

"*There* you are!" An elderly white-haired gentleman, a wide grin splitting his tanned face into a thousand wrinkles, burst into the room. He clapped Jared on the back, peered at Beth over Jenna's shoulder, and then eyed Melanie with an expression she could only interpret as sympathetic. "You must be Will's friend from Washington. Glad to meet you."

She took the hand he offered. "And you must be Uncle Joe."

He nodded, releasing her fingers after giving them a gentle squeeze of approval. "That's right, darlin'. Tell me something, do you play bridge?"

Before Melanie could answer, Jenna spoke. "Let the kids sit down and eat. You can arrange your card games over supper."

Melanie saw Jared peer into another room. "Where's Aunt Bitty?"

"Having a nap, I guess," Joe declared. "With that idiotic dog of hers."

"We'd better wake her up and tell her you're here or she'll have a fit," Jenna said.

"She can't hear a damn thing with those headphones on," the older man grumbled.

Jenna handed the baby to Melanie. "What's her name?"

"Beth."

"Well, bring Beth over here to the couch and get her settled. I know I have a cradle up in the attic Jared can get after supper, but for now we'll make do with pillows, all right?" She led Melanie past a round pedestal table set for supper to the other end of the room, where an overstuffed couch sat against a wall. A fuzzy brown afghan was spread over its back and blue towels covered the cushions. "I keep this old thing here so the men don't have to change their clothes in the middle of a workday when they want to sit down for a bit," she explained. "I saw a show on television explaining how to make slipcovers but I haven't tried it myself. What do you think for fabric, blue brushed corduroy or tan? I bought both because I couldn't make up my mind."

"Either one would work," she said, visualizing the old couch covered with new fabric. "You could do the couch in tan and then make pillows with the blue, if you wanted to bring that color into the room." Melanie sat down and laid Beth on her back on the middle cushion. The baby blinked at her as if to say *Where am I now?* "You're on a ranch," she told her. "No more trains or trucks for a little while."

"You poor thing. You must be exhausted and I'm rattling on about decorating." Jenna leaned over and helped unwrap Beth's blankets. "Let's get this little sweetheart settled."

"I could help you," Melanie said. "I worked for an interior designer for a couple of years after college, so I love talking about fabric and I'm a pretty good seamstress. Do you have a sewing machine?"

"Yes, but—"

She smiled at Will's mother. "Good. I may not have made you a grandmother, but I can make you a slipcover."

JARED STAYED by the door, then reached for his coat. He needed some air, especially after witnessing his mother's brief euphoria over the thought of having a grandchild. "I'm going back out to get the rest of Melanie's things."

"You need help, son?"

"I'm all set." The last thing he wanted was for Joe to catch pneumonia, though the man was as tough as any forty-year old he'd ever met. Still, there was no sense taking chances. "Just open the door when you see me coming."

Joe looked out the window at the falling snow. "Boy, we've got ourselves a white Christmas now, for sure."

"Yeah. I wish Will was here, though. If this keeps up he might have trouble getting home tomorrow." Which was not something Jared wanted to dwell on.

His uncle stepped closer and lowered his voice. "What's she like, this Melanie girl?"

He shrugged on his coat but didn't bother to zip it shut. "Nice enough, I guess."

"You spent hours with her and that's all you have to say, 'nice enough'?"

"What do you want me to say?" *Every protective urge I never knew I had has rushed through my body and clogged my brain and I want to carry that woman up to my bed and make love to her until she smiles at me again?* He wondered what his eighty-two-year-old uncle would say to that. Ready to make his escape, Jared kept one hand on the doorknob.

"I dunno. Maybe reveal a little conversation. You must have learned something about her."

"Not really."

"Do you know anything about the baby's father?"

"You're asking questions of the wrong man, Uncle Joe. You'll have to save them for Will." He turned away, but Joe wasn't finished talking.

"She's a pretty little thing." Joe seemed to be waiting for Jared to agree with him, so he nodded before turning back to open the door.

"Yes. If you like the type." The snow had covered the truck already, but he could still see their footprints leading to the porch.

"The type? What the hell does that mean? Young folks," Joe grumbled, waving him away. Jared stepped outside into the storm. He would get Melanie's suitcases and check on the horses before supper. All he needed was some fresh air and he would forget the ridiculous urge to take Melanie Briggs into his arms.

3

IT ALMOST WORKED, TOO. Until dinner, that is, when he made the mistake of touching her.

Jared hoped no one noticed when Melanie dropped her napkin and he, seated on her left, bent over to pick it up at the same time she leaned to get it herself. Her head hit his shoulder, her soft hair brushed his face, her fingers grabbed his arm when she thought she'd lost her balance.

"Oops," she said, righting herself. "Sorry."

"I've got it," he grumbled, trying real hard to ignore his physical reaction. He felt the heat in his face and didn't look at her when he handed her the square of white cloth. For some unknown reason his mother had stopped using paper napkins. He made a pretense of reaching for the salt shaker and caught a glimpse of Uncle Joe's hawk-eyed interest, but ignored it.

His mother cleared her throat.

"Jared," she began, forcing him to look up from a mound of mashed potatoes. "After dinner, could you go up in the attic and find our old cradle? I think there might be a playpen up there, too, but I'm not sure."

"I'll look," he said, forking another chunk of roast beef. He'd noticed that Melanie was close to cleaning her plate, which was impressive. She looked like one of those women who consumed nothing but carrot sticks, and yet she ate like a trucker.

Jenna turned to her left, where Aunt Bitty was busy slipping pieces to Fluffy. The dog knew enough to be quiet and stay close to Bitty's chair, and Jenna knew enough to ignore the subterfuge. "Aunt Bitty, do you remember that cradle? I think your father made it."

"Not my father," Bitty said, wiping her fingers on her napkin. "Raymond didn't know a handsaw from a piece of sandpaper. He'd rather have worked with horses than with wood, that's for sure."

Uncle Joe nodded. "I remember that. He had quite a knack, too. Melanie, honey, can you pass me those rolls? And the strawberry jelly, too, if you would."

Bitty slipped another piece of meat under the table and continued. "It was Jared's grandfather who liked building things, but he didn't do much of it. Didn't have the time."

Jared turned to Melanie to explain. "There've been four generations of Stones on this property, including Aunt Bitty's father, who was one of my grandfather's two brothers."

"Not very prolific, though," the old woman grumbled. "My father, Raymond Montrose Stone, just had the one girl. Me. And I never met a man I could stand for more than a few hours. Peter and Ethel's son died in Korea and their girls married and moved to Billings, but they're divorced now, you know."

Jared wondered how the hell he could get her to stop before she got down to the fact that he and Will needed to come up with some children of their own. "Aunt Bitty, has Mom shown you the Animal Planet channel yet?"

"Oh, pooh," she said, waving her hand at him. "She's always watching those craft shows. Yesterday we saw how to paint glasses and dishes, but you couldn't put 'em in the dishwasher, so what good are they?"

"Not much, I suspect," Joe supplied, giving Melanie a wink.

"Where was I?" Bitty frowned.

"Crafts," Jenna prompted.

"Oh, yes, the lack of descendants." Clearly Bitty was not going to be deterred. "Jenna and George, Jr. had the two boys, of course, which was exactly what the place needed."

Jared looked at his mother and silently mouthed *help*. She shrugged and let Bitty finish her ramblings, which were going to end up—as they always did— with the deplorable lack of family responsibility on his and Will's parts because they hadn't sowed their oats all over the county and sprouted future Graystone ranch hands.

"But the boys," she said, pausing to sigh dramatically. "The boys have not married and produced the next generation of Stones. Preferably male. And lots of them." She shot Melanie an apologetic look. "Not that I have anything against girls, my dear, but it takes *men* to run a place like this. *Married* men whose women know how to work, too. My mother could ride and rope with the best of them. Jenna, too. Do you ride, Melanie?"

"I actually preferred cooking to horses," Jenna interjected, much to Jared's relief. "Melanie, would you like some more roast beef? Jared, pass that platter over to her. The potatoes, too."

He did exactly that, holding the platter while Melanie took another slice of meat.

"Thank you." She gave him a small smile. "Please. Call me 'Mel.' Everyone does."

"They do?" The name didn't fit. He knew an auctioneer named Mel. He could spit a stream of tobacco twelve feet.

"Don't you have a nickname?"

"No."

Jared set the platter down and tried to think of something interesting to say as he handed her the bowl of mashed potatoes. The family was used to Bitty's comments and questions, but he hated the idea of Melanie being embarrassed. She didn't look embarrassed, though. She looked as if she wanted to laugh, as if she was enjoying herself. Odd. Aunt Bitty didn't usually inspire that sort of reaction.

"Looks like we're going to get a lot of snow tonight," was all he could manage to say. Everyone looked at him as if he'd just spoken Greek. "I...we won't be able to give Melanie—Mel—a tour of the ranch until the weather clears," he added. There. He gave Uncle Joe a *say something* look.

"Well—" the old man stopped buttering his roll and grinned at their guest "—tomorrow we'll have to plow a path to the barn and introduce you to the horses. Too bad that little baby of yours is too little to enjoy the animals."

"Yes, but I'll look forward to seeing everything," she said, glancing toward the couch where the child slept hemmed in by pillows. "I've never been to Montana before."

"We'll have to give you the grand tour, won't we, Jared?" Uncle Joe winked.

"Mrs. Stone, dinner is delicious."

"Call me Jenna, remember? What on earth did you eat on the train?"

"Sandwiches, mostly. Getting to the dining car was difficult with the baby."

That was probably an understatement, Jared figured.

Jenna was obviously fascinated. "So how did you manage?"

"The man who sat across from us—he was going all the way to Seattle—brought back food and coffee, which helped so much. People were very kind, but it

was a much harder trip than I thought it would be."
She wiped her lips with her napkin.

"Then why," Bitty asked, her three chins shaking,
"did you attempt such a thing?"

"I don't like to fly. Will didn't tell you?"

"Will didn't tell us much at all," Jared said, frowning. "Except that you had a red coat."

"I've never liked flying, either," Uncle Joe declared. "Give me my Ford truck any day. Seems like if I can't drive there I've got no business trying to get there in the first place."

"Folks gallivant around too much these days,"
Bitty added, giving Jared a disapproving look. "If the young people stayed home they'd most likely get married faster and start having sons. My folks were nineteen when they got married and seems like you'd better get busy and—"

"Who wants coffee? Or tea?" His mother stood and began to clear the dishes from the table, and Melanie leaped up to help her. Fluffy barked for leftovers, distracting Bitty from her latest lecture and saving Jared from having to grit his teeth and remind his aunt that thirty-two was not over the hill.

And then there was Melanie. Jared picked up his dishes and grabbed Joe's to take over to the sink, but he couldn't help noticing that Melanie—Mel—seemed real comfortable in the kitchen. She and Jenna were good-naturedly arguing over Mel's decision to wash the dishes, but then the baby cried and settled the argument. Melanie—he couldn't think of her as Mel—rushed over to pick up the child and coo into her ear.

Jared's heart sank down to his silver belt buckle. Was Will in love with her? Or worse, was she in love with Will? Why else travel by train—which sounded like the trip from hell—to spend the holidays with him?

"Jared." His mother put her hand on his arm and whispered, "What's the matter?"

"Nothing." He faked a yawn. "I guess I'm tired."

You couldn't fool Jenna Stone. She looked toward Melanie, who was bent over the couch putting the baby back in its makeshift nest. "She's very lovely."

"I guess."

"The baby isn't Will's, so whose is it? And where is he?"

"You'll have to wait until Will gets home to get the answers, Mom."

"Thank God that happens tomorrow," she said, keeping her voice low. "But I'm calling him tonight, right after dessert."

"Good idea." *And let me know what you find out.* If he was lusting after his future sister-in-law, he damned well wanted to know.

"What do you think?" Jenna had been anxious to talk to Joe since dinner, but there'd been dishes to wash, pie to serve and a guest who needed to get settled into bed before she fainted dead away from exhaustion. Bitty and Fluffy were upstairs listening to Dr. Laura on the radio and Jared had hustled off to hide in the barn.

"I think the boys can take care of themselves," her uncle declared. He folded up the newspaper and set it aside. "But it's no good telling you that because you're going to worry, anyway."

She folded her arms across her chest. "You saw the way he looked at her."

"Jared?" At her nod he continued, "Yes. She's a beautiful young woman. And if I was fifty or sixty years younger I might be looking at her like that, too."

"But—"

"He's a red-blooded man."

"And she's Will's."

"You don't know that."

"But he asked her here."

"Doesn't mean he's serious about her, Jenna." His voice grew gentle and he patted the space beside him on the leather couch. She crossed the room and sat down, then tucked her head against his shoulder.

"I know, but I worry." The den was one of her favorite rooms in the house—and the oldest. She loved the old leather furniture and her mother-in-law's braided rug; she had even grown fond of the elk antlers that graced the wall above the fireplace mantel. The fieldstone fireplace had kept generations of ranchers warm at night and was the place where the boys always hung their Christmas stockings, even though the tree stood in a corner of the much grander living room across the hall. She'd intended to get the tree after Will returned, so her sons would humor her and help decorate it.

"And I miss George." She'd loved that man since her thirteenth birthday when he delivered the collie pup her parents had gotten for her from the Stone ranch. He'd been gone eight years and sometimes it felt like forever.

"Yep. G.W. was a good man." He'd been "G.W.," short for George William, to a generation of older men who'd known Jenna's father-in-law as George and called his son by his initials to avoid confusion.

"He'd know what to do. Will would have told him all about this girl." She felt the beginning of a headache coming on.

"If there was something to tell," her uncle reminded her.

"I just wish I knew what was going on. I called Will but there was no answer. I got his damn voice mail again."

"He'll call back."

"He'd better do it soon. It's getting late and I wanted to warn him about the storm."

"As if you have to tell a cattleman about the weather."

She chuckled. "I have a few more things to talk

about than the weather. Such as, is he serious about Melanie and where is the father of that baby?"

"She's a pretty little thing, that baby is. Doesn't cry much."

"I thought she was my granddaughter when they walked in the door tonight. Part of me still wishes she was."

"Nothing wrong with wishful thinking," the old man declared. "But there isn't a Stone man—dead or alive—who wouldn't have married the mother of his child. Your Will's cut from the same cloth.

"Jared, too." Uncle Joe nodded his agreement. Jenna lifted her head to look at him. "You saw his face tonight, didn't you?"

"He passed her the potatoes."

Jenna sighed and lifted herself off the couch. She crossed the room and added another log to the fire. Her temples began to throb in earnest. "I think I'm going to take some aspirin and go to bed."

"You do that, hon. I think I'll wait for Jared to finish up in the barn and see if I can get him to play a hand of rummy. Where's our houseguest? In bed for the night?"

"Settled in with the baby upstairs." She stepped over to the window and pulled the drape back. The lights were still on in the large barn, meaning Jared was taking his sweet time doing chores. "Damn snow."

Joe picked up his newspaper. "Go to bed and quit your worryin'."

Good advice, of course, but easier said than done. She crossed the foyer and, careful to keep from making too much noise, headed up the stairs. Tomorrow she would decorate the banister with pine boughs and big red bows. Maybe Melanie would like to help. She seemed like the kind of young woman who enjoyed being useful, but her presence here could be a problem.

She couldn't explain it to Joe. Not this. Jared had looked at Melanie just like his father had looked at her that night when she was sixteen and had been alone in the horse barn with him. George had kissed her—*really* kissed her—for the first time. The secret love of her life finally looked at her as if he'd never seen anyone so beautiful. And she was not a raving beauty, not then and not ever. But George—all grown up at the ripe old age of twenty-three—thought she was. And looked at her as if he wanted to do all those things men did with women in the romance books she'd loved reading. On her eighteenth birthday, two weeks after she'd graduated from high school, they spent a honeymoon weekend in Great Falls and she'd discovered that books couldn't compare with the real thing.

Jenna paused at the top of the stairs. The upper level was shaped like a *T*, with her wing on the left, the boys' rooms on the right and the long corridor lined with guest rooms. She used to joke that she could open a bed-and-breakfast and make extra money, if all else failed. A hundred years or so ago the Stones used all this space, but now it seemed wasteful to let them go empty. She heard the radio behind Bitty's closed door, but it wasn't likely to disturb the others, since Bitty's was the first room off the stairs. Uncle Joe and Melanie were opposite each other four doors down, with Melanie using the guest room that had its own bathroom.

The baby was fussing. Jenna paused and wondered if she should knock and offer to help, but decided that the young mother could no doubt use some privacy. It wasn't as if little Beth was her own granddaughter, after all.

And it wasn't as if the pretty dark-haired woman was Jared's "special" guest. Her oldest son, far more serious and quiet than Will, didn't lose his heart easily. In fact, she wondered if he ever had.

Jenna entered her bedroom, recently redecorated in shades of white and cream, and prayed neither one of her boys would get hurt.

EVEN WHEN SHE LAY SNUGGLED under the covers, Melanie still felt as if she was on the train. Not that she'd been horizontal under a pink-and-purple flannel comforter on the train, of course, but when she closed her eyes she could almost feel the rumble of the tracks under the bed.

Beth fussed in her cradle, so Melanie stretched her arm down to rock the little pine bed. Jared, strong and silent and oh-so-capable, had carried it down from the attic, wiped it clean and proceeded to fold blankets to create a soft mattress.

He'd said one word. "There."

She'd thanked him and he'd stridden out of her bedroom and shut the door behind him as if he wished she'd stayed put, behind a closed door, until it was time for her to go home. Obviously he thought she was here to claim his brother and he didn't approve. And yet he'd been kind to her. Once again she'd had the strangest urge to throw herself into his arms and lean on that wide chest and hang on for dear life.

Hormones, of course, were her major problem. Not feelings of attraction for Will's older brother. She blamed everything else on hormones, why not this?

Mel eyed the small brass clock on the nightstand. After midnight, which meant she'd been asleep for almost two hours. Beth's fussing meant she would want to nurse again soon and Melanie felt the familiar heaviness in her breasts that came every four hours or so.

Sure enough, Beth let out a screech that wouldn't be appeased by the rocking of her bed, and Mel scooped her up into the soft double bed, plumped the pillows against the oak headboard and fed her while snow pelted the windows on the far side of the room.

She had made the right decision by coming here. No one here felt sorry for her—if she didn't count understandable sympathy about traveling by train with an infant. No one in this self-sufficient family felt guilty about celebrating Christmas while Melanie mourned a fiancé who died nine months ago when a plane crashed into a Kansas cornfield. No concerned relative with worried eyes had whispered, "But what are you going to do *now*?"

And while she loved her aunt and uncle and their daughter, Dylan, who was most likely furious with her, she didn't intend to ruin their Christmas.

She didn't intend to ruin anyone's Christmas.

FOR ONE SPINE-CHILLING SECOND Jared thought the house was haunted. The soundless moving of the rocking chair, the light-colored gown, the glare of snow coming in through the living room windows and a sudden keening cry all added up to a good reason for his heart to end up in his throat.

Just for a second, of course.

But the ghostly vision was Melanie in a long robe, rocking a fussy baby in Grandmother Stone's favorite chair.

He swore under his breath. Couldn't the woman stay put in her own room?

Her eyes widened as she saw him. "I'm sorry," she whispered. "Did we wake you? I thought if we came downstairs—"

"No. I came down for something to eat." He kept his voice low, though he didn't know why he bothered. The baby was clearly not going to go to sleep. It kept lifting its head from its mother's shoulder and making frustrated noises. "That is one angry kid you've got there."

"No kidding." She surprised him by smiling, which didn't help his resolve to ignore her. "She didn't get her temper from me, I swear."

Then from whom? He didn't voice the question aloud. It wasn't his business. None of this was his business. "I thought rocking chairs were supposed to make babies go to sleep."

"Tell *her* that." Mel leaned forward and lifted herself from the chair. Her robe, a pale shade of green, looked soft. It was tied at her waist with satin strings and hung to her ankles. And she was barefoot.

"I didn't want to make any noise," she explained when she caught him looking at her feet.

"You'll catch cold. Come into the den and I'll get a fire going." He was insane, he reminded himself. He should get back to his own room, take the stairs two at a time, lock the door. Damn Will, anyway.

"It's almost two o'clock," she protested, patting the baby's back. The infant squirmed against her and let out a little cry. But her head settled on Mel's shoulder. "We'd better try going back to bed."

"Suit yourself," he murmured, trying not to look at the triangle of skin revealed between the satin lapels of her robe. Lace peeked up from her nightgown. "I'm going to find out where my mother hid the Christmas cookies."

"Really?" Her face lit up and she took a step toward the door as if she was going to follow him, but she tripped and pitched forward.

He caught her by the forearms before she crashed to the floor. She was against his chest, the baby's head under his chin, Mel's soft breasts against his T-shirt. Thank goodness he'd shoved on jeans before coming downstairs. He took a deep breath but didn't release her. Her hair smelled like vanilla, he noted. And she was leaning against him.

Her forehead was against his chest, and he felt her body relax as he released her arms and slid his hands to her back. He wondered how long it had been since someone had held her.

"Are you okay?"

"Just stubbed my toe, that's all."

"It's the braided rugs," he explained. "They're old and uneven. I should throw them out."

"I'll be more careful."

Yes, he thought, watching her head up the stairs. *We both should.*

4

"WILL MISSED HIS PLANE."

This Tuesday morning news was greeted as if Jenna had announced that a giant asteroid was going to hit the ranch in five seconds. Bitty clutched her dog to her chest and moaned. Jared muttered something under his breath, and Jenna looked as if she wanted to burst into tears. Melanie, holding Beth, stood in the doorway of the kitchen and waited to see what would happen next. She was disappointed, of course, but surely Will would be here as soon as he could. And there were still eight days before Christmas.

"Well, damn," Joe said. "I just finished plowing the road."

"How the hell could he miss his plane?" This was from Jared. "He was supposed to get an eleven o'clock flight out of Dulles."

Jenna shrugged. "He didn't give any details, and he said he'd call back when he got another flight. There's one at six-thirty tonight on Delta, but he said something about trying to get an earlier plane on a different airline."

"Jeez."

Then the four of them looked at Melanie as if she might have the answers. She patted the baby's back and made her way around the kitchen table to an empty seat. "Maybe there was a lot of traffic on the way to the airport."

"Did Will call you, too?" Jenna set a cup of coffee on the table in front of her. "What did he say?"

"Uh, nothing. I mean, he didn't call." There was no reason to explain that she kept her cell phone turned off most of the time and only used it when absolutely necessary. But when she opened her mouth to explain that she and Will were friends and not about to be anything else, Uncle Joe—he'd told her to call him that—interjected his own thoughts on the situation.

"Well," he drawled, "I s'pose we'll see him when we see him and that's that. At least we know he's on his way. Are we playing cards tonight? Melanie, do you know how to play bridge?"

"I learned how in college, but that was a while ago."

Uncle Joe grinned. "That's enough, honey. We'll get us a game together tonight while Jared here goes to the airport. Jenna plays and Bitty can be talked into it as long as she stays awake."

Jenna set a plate of buttered toast in front of Melanie. "I'm sure Will will let us know when he's coming, even if it's late tonight. Why don't you get the Christmas tree today instead of tomorrow?" This question was directed at Jared. "Take Melanie with

you and show her around town. She hasn't seen
much of Montana except for snow."

Melanie shook her head. "I can't—"

"Of course you can. I'd be happy to baby-sit,"
Jenna said. "You won't be gone very long—in between feedings—and I'd love to hold her. We'll
watch the home-decorating channel and learn how to
make broken-tile mosaic planters for Christmas
gifts." She smiled and patted Melanie's shoulder. "I
remember what it was like to try to shop with a baby
in tow. And don't tell me you don't need a little break
from motherhood."

"Well..." She needed a little break from Jared, who
pointedly ignored the conversation and instead
reached for his jacket. It hadn't been easy going back
to sleep last night after making such a fool of herself.
She'd been embarrassed for leaning against him, for
succumbing to that moment when she'd yearned to
be held.

"You can stop at the store and pick up some more
flour and eggs for me," Jenna said. "I'm still not done
with baking and—" she looked at Joe "—someone's
been sneaking the cookies I put away for Christmas."

"Just once," the elderly man confessed. "Maybe
twice. They're real good, too, especially those candy
cane ones."

"Fluffy likes the sugar cookies." Bitty didn't look
the least bit guilty. "I ran out of his dog treats."

"Write up a list and I'll get whatever you need,"

Jared said, then looked at Melanie as if he couldn't decide if he wanted her back in the truck with him again. And as much as she wanted to see Montana in the daylight, being alone with the man could be a little uncomfortable. She thought about going into his arms last night and hoped that the heat in her face didn't mean she was blushing. It was odd, having that kind of reaction to a man who was little more than a stranger. *You'll like Jared,* Will had said. *You can trust him.*

"I wouldn't mind helping get groceries," she heard herself say.

"Good." Jenna patted Melanie's shoulder. "Don't be shy about doing any last-minute Christmas shopping, either. Duggan isn't a very big town, but there's a hardware store, a couple of restaurants, a bookstore, one place that sells clothing—if you like jeans and boots—and a few other shops you might find interesting. Make sure you get to Burger Barn for lunch. We're very proud of our Montana beef."

"Why don't you come with us?"

The older woman laughed. "No way. I'm staying here and pretending I'm a grandma. And I want to stick around to answer the phone when Will calls again. You two go ahead and have fun. Just make sure Jared doesn't buy a tree that's bigger than the living room."

"All right." Since the living room was twice the

size of her entire apartment, Melanie didn't think that would be a problem.

Jared looked back at her before he walked out the door. "When do you want to leave?"

"In an hour?" That would give her time to bathe and feed the baby. It was a gorgeous sunny day, bright blue sky contrasting with the snow-covered ground. The thought of going outside in the sunshine, no matter how cold the temperature, was tempting. The thought of shopping for an hour or two without Beth was so irresistible she fought a pang of guilt.

"Fine. Dress warm." With that piece of advice said, Jared hurried out the door as if he couldn't wait to leave.

She supposed a rancher's work was never done.

"MY, MY, HONEY." Uncle Joe winked at her as he helped himself to a piece of Martha Stewart's special recipe for coffee cake. "I get the feelin' you're up to something."

Jenna helped herself to a small slice of cranberry cake. The baby, asleep in her arms, was blissfully unaware that her mother had just gone off Christmas shopping. "We needed a tree, that's all."

"I could have gotten you one," her uncle pointed out, a grin splitting his wrinkled face. "You didn't have to send the young folks—unless you had something else in mind."

She adjusted the sleeping child against the crook of her left elbow, then took a bite of cake. "I like holding babies. And my oldest son is lonely. And—"

"And last night you were worried that your boys might like the same woman," he interjected. "'Course, I told you that was nonsense. I guess you decided to take my advice, huh?"

"I was going to say that since we have a lovely young woman here, what's wrong with a little match-making?" Jenna looked down at little Beth. If she had any kind of a father she'd be with him for the holidays. So obviously Beth and her mommy were alone. And what was wrong with wanting Jared to be happy? Will, the outgoing one, shuttled back and forth to D.C. and involved himself in making the world a better place for ranchers like himself. In his job as a lobbyist with a crop-protection agency he met women constantly, and Jenna had no doubt he'd broken the hearts of sweet young things wearing little black cocktail dresses. Jared was content to stay in Montana and take care of business at home, which didn't leave time for finding the woman of his dreams. "I've decided to be an equal-opportunity mother."

"What the hell does that mean?"

"Shh." She glanced down to see the baby was still sleeping soundly before turning back to Joe. "Will's had his chance with Melanie. In Washington. Now it's Jared's turn."

"Fair enough," Joe said. "But I, uh, don't think Will's gonna—"

"Oh, for heaven's sake," Aunt Bitty sputtered, shuffling into the kitchen with Fluffy wriggling in her arms. "Those boys will figure it out. One of them had better marry that young woman and give that baby a father." She put Fluffy on the floor, then sat down in the chair next to Joe. She nodded when she saw that Jenna held the baby. "We need more of those around here."

"You don't think Will's going to *what?*"

"I don't think he's gonna mind if Jared falls for that little gal," the old man said. "I was just thinkin' out loud, that's all."

"You ever rent that movie, *Legends of the Fall?*" Bitty offered the dog a piece of cake, but he ignored her and trotted over to Jenna's chair to sniff a corner of the baby's blanket.

"Be nice, Fluffy," Jenna told him, though the old dog didn't seem to be anything more than curious. He probably wondered why he wasn't in someone's lap, too.

"The one where the sons all fall in love with the same woman and everyone winds up dead?" This was from Joe, who was proud of his DVD collection. "Good Lord, Bitty, what are you getting at?"

"Oh, hush," she said, eating the piece of cake herself. "It's not like I said you were Anthony Hopkins or going to have a stroke or anything like that. I'm just trying to suggest that this matchmaking thing had better be done right or there could be a real disaster."

"Now I'm worried all over again," Jenna said, though her dark-haired sons were much better-looking than Brad Pitt. Taller, too.

Joe glared at Bitty. "Shouldn't you be listenin' to your radio shows or something, instead of spreading doom and gloom?"

"Dr. Laura's on vacation," she said. "Or I'd call her for advice."

"Common sense is what folks need nowadays," Joe declared. "Not more radio shows."

"You call playing cards all day having common sense?"

"Stop, both of you," Jenna said, keeping her voice low. "No arguing in front of the baby. If she wakes up it will be both your faults."

"Well," Bitty said, clapping her hands to attract Fluffy to her. "It's as if fate has stepped in, anyway, with Will being late."

"Like it was meant to be," Joe agreed, looking at Jenna for confirmation.

And then the phone rang.

WELL, DAMN. ANY IDEA he had of making a quick trip to town was evaporating. The woman was having one hell of a good time at Jorgensen's Western Wear. She didn't seem too upset that his brother was delayed, which he thought odd. You'd think she'd be pining away for him, her hand clutched to a cell phone awaiting its ring.

But no. She'd spent time debating which small blanket to buy for her daughter: the one with galloping horses or the one with a Navajo design. She'd browsed the small bookstore on the corner of Central Avenue, purchased an array of baby necessities at the IGA while he'd located dog treats and the things on his mother's grocery list, and chatted with the owner of a secondhand store about vintage fabrics and antique quilts. Jared got the impression it was something Melanie knew quite a bit about, because Betty Stevens brought out three different old brown patchwork quilts from under the counter and asked her opinion.

While the women talked, Jared found an old poker chip holder, complete with red, blue and white handmade chips, for Joe. He'd finish the rest of his shopping in Great Falls when he went to the airport. Melanie purchased a tablecloth, which she said was for Jenna, and one of the quilts.

"What are you going to do with that?" he couldn't help asking. He'd never seen a worse-looking quilt, unless he counted the ones in the bunkhouse. He couldn't picture sleeping under it. Unless, of course, Melanie Briggs was under the covers with him. He supposed in that case he'd sleep under month-old newspapers.

"I'm torn," she confessed, looking pleased. "It's a Christmas present, but I'd love to keep it myself."

He avoided pointing out that it smelled like a root cellar and the edges were coming apart. Women were funny about criticism, and besides, he was glad she seemed to be having such a good time. When they stepped outside she didn't seem to mind the cold wind that threatened to knock her over. He even put his hand on her elbow to help her over a ridge of plowed snow at the edge of the parking lot.

Of course, touching her was tempting. And before the day was over he intended to find out what she and Will had going, because when his brother arrived in the airport lobby and after they said "Hey, how are you?" he intended to start asking questions.

He drove to the Burger Barn, which was next door to the lot where Christmas trees were lined up against the side of the Texaco station. The local preschool mothers were holding a bake sale inside the garage, so he bought a carrot cake and a tray of muffins and donated an extra twenty dollars to the search-and-rescue fund. Melanie insisted on purchasing a tray of cookies cut out in the shape of Santa Claus and decorated with red and white frosting and then discussed babies with a young woman whose infant was tucked against her chest in some contraption that looked like a sling.

"We'll get the tree after we eat," Jared said, when

the young mother with the baby waited on another customer. "Come on."

She followed him back to the truck, gave him her cookies to put in the back seat with the rest of the purchases, and then walked beside him across the parking lot to the small box-shaped restaurant. He watched her order a double-cheese burger, fries and a chocolate shake and ordered the same thing for himself. The woman could eat, all right.

"So," he began, when she looked around at the crowd gathered for lunch. "What did you think of Duggan?"

"I liked it. Everyone is so friendly here."

"Unlike Washington?"

"Different." The waitress brought their drinks and Melanie took her time unwrapping the straw. "People here aren't in a hurry. And everyone seems to know one another."

"True." As if to prove her point, two women Jenna's age waved at him. Jared nodded his hello and turned his attention back to Melanie. She looked less tired today. Her cheeks matched the red of her jacket, and the dark circles under her eyes were lighter. "What do you do there?"

"I work part-time with my cousin. She's an interior designer."

"That's what you are? A designer?" He was surprised. Melanie didn't look like the artsy-sophisticated type he thought a "designer" would be.

She took a sip of her chocolate shake and looked euphoric, as if she would burst into song. "I work behind the scenes. My specialty is vintage fabric and I do a lot of special-order work. In other words," she said, in between sips, "I sew."

Now he understood the appeal of the ragged quilt. Sort of. "So when you told my mother you'd help her cover the couch, you weren't kidding."

"It's going to be a lot easier than she thinks." She took another sip of her drink. "This is the best chocolate shake I've had in my life."

"So," he drawled, in what he hoped could be interpreted as casual. "How did you meet my brother?"

"He sublet the apartment next to mine."

That must have been cozy. "Yeah. Will hates hotels."

"That's what he told me. But he said he likes traveling to Washington and he likes his work there." The waitress returned with their hamburger plates. Melanie looked at her watch. "I hope your mother is doing okay with Beth."

"She's in heaven," he promised. "I don't imagine your baby has been out of her arms."

"I left a bottle of formula in case Beth gets hungry before we get back, but I shouldn't stay away too much longer."

"All we have left to do is get a tree," he assured her. And she smiled at him, something that caused his body to react with startling need.

No, he decided, looking down at his lunch. It was easier to think of her as a woman who belonged somewhere else. To someone else. He didn't want to watch her talking to everyone she met and smiling as if she had never had so much fun or eating a hamburger as if it were from a four-star D.C. restaurant. He didn't want to like her, unless it was more of a brotherly kind of affection than the frequent desire to haul her into his arms and let the rest of the world go to hell.

HELPING JARED PICK OUT the perfect Christmas tree turned out to be the hardest thing she'd done all day—except for attempting to wake up at dawn, when Beth was screaming for an early breakfast. A handmade sign read Your Choice, Twenty Dollars, carols blared from an outside speaker, and once in a while someone would honk their car horn and Jared would look toward the gas pumps and wave.

She couldn't think of anything else she'd rather do than pick out Beth's first Christmas tree.

"This one looks okay," Jared said, holding it out for her inspection.

"I see a bare spot," she pointed out as he held out a particularly tall fir. "Right there in the back."

He turned it, nodded and set it back against the cement wall.

Melanie pointed to a fat, shorter tree a few yards away. "What about that one?"

"Too short" was his reply, but he went over and lifted it away from the wall to look at it better.

"But your mother said—"

"She always says she doesn't want a big tree, but she doesn't mean it."

Melanie stuck her nose close to a fat branch and inhaled the scent of pine. "Nothing smells better than a Christmas tree." She hummed along with "Rudolph the Red-Nosed Reindeer." "This is so much fun. Doesn't it give you the Christmas spirit?"

He gave her an odd look before replacing the tree alongside the others they'd rejected. "I suppose. My mother has a militant approach to tree-decorating. Will and I usually find chores to do in the barn."

"Coward."

"Call me names after you've survived the experience, sweetheart."

Sweetheart?

He cleared his throat. "You're not cold?"

"Not yet," she fibbed, wishing she'd worn two pairs of socks inside her boots instead of one. She should have bought long underwear at Jorgensen's when she'd had the chance, because her jeans were freezing against her skin. Her leather gloves weren't nearly warm enough, so she kept her hands in her pockets. "I think we should keep looking."

Jared walked farther down toward the back corner of the building, Melanie close behind. She was a little surprised he was so patient. Her uncle, sweet but thrifty to a fault, had always picked out inexpensive, scrawny trees until he and Aunt Lillian bought an artificial tree a few years ago. Peter had been relieved, but Dylan had had a genuine fit. *Tradition,* she'd said, *should be more important than convenience.* Aunt Lillian had laughed and hugged her, and then continued decorating her six-foot artificial pine. None of them would be pleased with her decision to spend the holidays away from them.

"Mel."

She looked up to see Jared holding another tree.

"Daydreaming?" he asked.

"A little. I was thinking about my uncle Peter and his choice of Christmas trees. My poor aunt always had such a hard time putting the lights on and making it look good." She fought an unfamiliar wave of homesickness and thought she would call her cousin this afternoon. She'd apologize for running away and she'd tell Dylan she'd bought her a Christmas present she wouldn't be able to resist.

"What do you think of this one?"

Melanie stepped closer and walked around the tree. It was bushy and thick, with dark green needles and a fragrant odor of pine. "I don't see any empty spots, but is it too tall?"

"No. I can always cut some off the bottom if it is." He looked down at her and smiled, surprising her. She didn't think he smiled often. Maybe he was the sort of person who didn't enjoy company. Maybe he didn't like babies. Or city girls.

Or women who tripped on rugs and landed in his arms in the middle of the night.

"What?" he said, frowning a little now.

"Nothing." She pretended to study the tree. Even though she was a mother now, she could still appreciate this handsome rancher. There was something about a man in jeans and cowboy boots that made her think of doing things a mother shouldn't be thinking of doing. Her body seemed to be coming alive now, as if her hormones had recovered from the pregnancy and were now shouting "Hey, Mel! We're back! Have you noticed?"

She'd noticed, all right. And she wasn't about to go roaming around the house at two o'clock in the morning again, that was certain.

5

THE BAD NEWS, JARED discovered upon arriving home, was that Will wasn't getting home anytime soon. He'd called to say he was stuck in Chicago and wasn't sure he'd be on that flight to Minneapolis as planned. The message to Jared was to "stand by," so Jared wouldn't make the trip to Great Falls for nothing.

So Jared would have to continue avoiding Melanie Briggs. He wasn't very good at avoiding her, though. He'd taken her to town, to lunch and home again. He'd spent the afternoon working in his office, and as soon as supper was over, he'd spend the evening doing chores in the horse barn.

The good news was that Melanie was busy with his mother, which meant that if he was careful, he need never spend more than thirty seconds alone with her. While he was filling out account books and breeding records, Melanie would be helping decorate the house for Christmas.

While he was feeding the cattle, Melanie could start sewing up that couch cover his mother was so thrilled about.

And when she was rocking her child in the middle

of the night, he would be sure to stay in his room. It was a good plan, an easy plan, the best plan for the next twenty-four hours.

Until Uncle Joe announced, "Jared, we need a fourth for bridge."

That night Will called to say there was a storm in Chicago, the same one that had roared through Montana on Monday. Flights were being canceled left and right and he'd call them in the morning as soon as he knew what he was going to do. And, he'd added to tease Jenna, he was having a little difficulty with their mother's Christmas gift, among other things.

Jared couldn't ask any questions about Will's relationship with Melanie, seeing how his mother and Joe were on the extensions. He tried later, but only reached Will's voice mail. On Wednesday he'd planned to spend the day in his office, so he answered Will's call and heard about the new travel plans. Will was renting a car, but he'd lost his wallet and needed money, and Jared was more than happy to wire him all he needed. "Just hurry home," he said, wanting to explain, but Aunt Bitty knocked on the door and asked for his help in the living room and Will said he had to go.

"Jared, my boy, we need you to get the ladder," she'd said, Fluffy panting at her ankles. He'd ended up spending the afternoon helping Melanie hang ornaments while Joe, with Fluffy on his lap, snored in the leather recliner and his mother and Bitty played with the baby.

ON THURSDAY MORNING Jenna took Aunt Bitty to town, Jared and Joe fixed a leak in the machine shop's roof and Melanie washed clothes, so unfortunately no one was around to answer the phone. Will left a message on the answering machine saying he was about to leave Davenport, Iowa, where he'd spent the night. He promised his mother he would be home for Christmas and asked Joe to make sure Melanie got to ride a horse.

Uncle Joe, complaining of a sudden and painful arthritis flare-up, reached for a heating pad and suggested that Jared saddle up Ralph, the oldest horse on the ranch, and told him not to forget to see that Melanie visited the original homestead. Later on that afternoon, Jenna fixed a thermos of spiced tea, Aunt Bitty wrapped up cookies in a plastic bag and Jared looked out the window and prayed for snow.

He could have said no. He should have said no. But Melanie looked at him with such delight that the objections clogged in his throat.

"Fine," he managed to croak. "When?"

"Beth just fell asleep, so I'm set for about three hours."

"That's plenty of time," Jenna declared. "Take my down jacket, Melanie, and one of the scarves hanging over there by the coatrack."

"But the cookies—"

"Will wait till later," his mother said. "We have plenty of days to bake."

"Are you sure?" Melanie directed this question to Jared.

He shrugged. "I don't mind."

Of course it was a lie. He minded one hell of a lot, just like he'd minded sitting across the table from her while they played cards. He'd minded holding the ladder steady so she could reach the high ornaments. That cute little rear of hers had been in full view, and what a view it was. She was completely feminine, from the top of her silky hair to her tiny feet and all the areas in between. She smelled good, had a smile that turned him inside out and she fit into his family as if she'd lived here forever.

Even Fluffy liked her.

Hell, Fluffy even liked the baby. The little white runt curled up on the floor next to whatever piece of furniture Beth was cocooned on unless he was coaxed away with offers of food.

She was the most dangerous woman he'd ever met.

THEY RODE FENCE FOR LESS than an hour, until it got too cold to be outside. He explained how this part of the ranch operated. He pointed out the old homestead, now used by the hands hired in the summer. He showed her the creek, told her stories of growing up with Will and the jokes they'd played on each other. She clung to the saddle horn at first, but after a while she got the hang of Ralph's gait and became easier in the saddle. By the time the wind came up and the sky darkened, they were safely in the barn unsaddling the horses.

"Is there something wrong, Jared?"

"Why?" He unbuckled the girth, lifted the saddle

and blanket from Ralph's back and draped them over a sawhorse.

"I think I must have done something to upset you."

He glanced back, which was a mistake. She stood close. Too close. Her knit hat covered her hair, but she'd removed the scarf from over her face and it hung over the front of her jacket. She looked younger than when he'd first seen her; her nose and cheeks were red and he knew if he touched her face it would be cold.

"No," he said. He moved toward the horse, and Melanie stepped out of his way.

"I seem to be in your way a lot," she said. "What can I do to help?"

"Nothing." He didn't mean to sound curt, but he was aware they were alone in a huge, warm building that smelled of hay and was completely private. He really needed to get off the ranch more. Call someone. Get a date. Go to the movies or something. He slid the bridle off Ralph's head and left the stall. This time he closed the door behind him. "I mean, thanks, but I've got it all under control. You can go back to the house if you want."

"I could help."

"I'm just going to rub the horses down." He hooked the bridle on a nail and picked up a brush.

"Show me?"

He wanted to swear. He wanted to turn her around to face the door and show her the way out, but touching her came with the usual problem of how to hide how she affected him. "You'll get filthy."

"I don't mind." She tilted her head and looked at him. "I think I'm ruining your Christmas and I don't know why. Whatever it is, I'm sorry."

"You're not ruining anything." Except his sleep. He walked past her and went back into the stall to give Ralph a good rubdown, and the damn woman followed him.

"I'm an unmarried woman with a baby. Is that it?"

Unmarried. Well, that was welcome news. Jared turned away from the horse, though Ralph was too busy eating fresh hay to care if he was getting brushed or not.

"That's your business," he said, watching her fidget with the ends of her scarf. "But how is Will involved?"

"Your brother was kind enough to invite me here for Christmas."

That was not what he meant when he asked, but Jared didn't ask the question again. She was close—too close—and if he wasn't careful it would be so easy to pull her into his arms and most likely scare her to death.

"This is a curry brush," he said, holding it out to her. She hurriedly removed her gloves and tucked them into the pockets of her coat before she took it. "You brush him down. And never get behind a horse, or even a mild animal like Ralph might kick."

"Okay." She stepped closer, but Jared stayed next to Ralph's head and hooked a rope onto his halter so he couldn't move around. He watched Melanie brush the animal's side with tentative strokes.

"How am I doing?" She looked over to grin at him and patted Ralph's neck. "I'm still a hopeless greenhorn, right?"

"You're doing fine." He was jealous of a damn horse. "You can switch sides. It's not like he got much of a workout today."

She scooted between him and the horse's chest, then started in on the other side. Jared didn't mind watching her.

"How do I know when I'm done?"

"When you smell like Ralph."

"I like the way he smells," she said, giving the horse's side a pat before she moved up to his head. She handed Jared the brush, then stood on tiptoe to give him a quick kiss on his cheek. He was so surprised that he didn't react.

"Thank you for taking me riding and for everything else," she said, a soft smile lighting her eyes. "You've been stuck with me for days and you've been really kind and really patient about this whole thing."

"Patient?" he choked out. When she would have moved toward the stall door, he dropped the brush in the straw and put his hands on her shoulders.

"Very," she whispered, gazing up at him with an expression he couldn't read. "Patient."

He lowered his head. There was not a damn thing that he could do about stopping himself, either, because he wasn't feeling very patient or kind at the moment. Her mouth tilted upward and when he touched his lips to hers she didn't move. He was only curious, he told himself. He wanted to know what it would be like to touch his mouth to hers.

Her lips were warmer than he thought they would be, but softer than he'd ever have been able to imagine. It was the merest brush of a kiss, for starters. A brief meeting of mouths meant to ease the ache inside, it deepened into something else.

Out of curiosity, of course. Nothing more.

Jared's hands left her shoulders, skimmed upward to cup her neck. His fingers swept under her hair and he slanted his mouth against hers.

She made a little sound and her hands gripped the front of his jacket when he urged her lips apart. His tongue touched hers, teased and flicked up and down inside her mouth. She tasted of sugar and almonds, of Christmas cookies and cinnamon tea.

He urged her closer, carefully, conscious of how fragile she felt under his hands. But not too close; his erection was blatant and unmistakable. If she felt him she would think he was going to tumble her into the hay. And he didn't want her to know how much she affected him with one simple kiss.

But nothing was simple, not the way she kissed him back, first hesitant, then hot, as if she could no more hide her reaction than he could. He made love to her mouth as if that was the only way he would ever do so. Wanting to taste her, wanting to please her, wanting to keep her.

Wanting to love her.

She was on tiptoe when he ended the kiss, leaning

against him and holding on to his jacket as if she would fall onto the cement floor otherwise.

"You started it," he said when he saw her open her mouth to speak. He figured she was going to say something and he was most likely going to have to apologize.

He'd be damned if he'd apologize. Not when she had smiled at him and kissed his cheek.

"Yes," she said. "I guess I did."

"Are you in love with my brother?" It was a blunt question, but as Jared caught his breath and willed his body to cool down, he had to know the answer. He expected the answer.

"No." Clearly the question surprised her. Those hazel eyes of hers looked dazed, and her face, usually so pale, was flushed. Her lips were full and swollen. Thoroughly kissed. "I'm not in love with anyone."

She brushed past him, out of the stall and toward the barn door. He saw her tie her scarf around her ears before she went outside into darkness that was the color of a winter afternoon.

Jared took his time brushing down his own horse and finishing the chores. He chipped ice from the water trough out in the corral and hoped the cold wind would act the way a cold shower was supposed to.

If she was his...well, he knew damn well what they'd be doing now instead of chores. They'd shower the horse smell off and tumble into his king-size bed and make love for an hour or two.

Or three.

Or at least until the baby cried. He was a realistic

man; he knew that babies cried and wanted to be fed. He knew that suppers burned and phones rang and relatives dropped in unannounced.

No, there would be no bed with Melanie in it. She might not be in love with his brother, but there was no way of knowing how Will felt about her. For all Jared knew, his brother was bent on making Mel the next Mrs. Stone.

And one thing brothers didn't do was poach on each other's women.

No, he would keep away from her. Far, far away from her. And if Will really was in love with this woman, then Jared would keep his guilt to himself and wish him well.

"HER PARENTS ARE DEAD, you know," Bitty said, dealing the next hand of gin. "Killed in a car crash when she was six."

"Well, the poor little gal," Joe said, ignoring the cards being dealt. "Jenna? Did you know that?"

"Not exactly." She stood at the kitchen window and looked toward the barn. The lights were on, meaning Jared and Melanie had returned from their ride, but they had been in the barn for quite a while. Not that it mattered, she knew, glancing toward the sofa to make sure the baby still slept. Beth had been a perfect angel, entertaining the three of them with her antics before she grew tired and fussed to be put down.

Joe blew his nose. "How the hell do you know all this?"

"I asked," Bitty said. "Simple as that."

"She didn't mind?"

"She didn't seem to. I said, 'Where are your folks for Christmas?' I figured she'd tell me her parents lived overseas or something. I was a little worried that she didn't get along with her family, which wouldn't have been a very good sign, if you ask me."

"I can't imagine Melanie not getting along with anyone," Jenna said, her gaze still on the barn.

"You could have knocked me over with Fluffy's tail when she told me she was raised by her aunt and uncle."

"Did she say anything about little Beth's father?" Joe asked.

"No, but she sure loves that baby of hers," Bitty said, and then the only sound was the slap of a card on the table top.

"They still in the barn?" Joe scraped his chair back and went over to stand beside Jenna. "Lights are on, huh?"

"Your idea might just be working," she told him. "Giving them privacy, a chance to get to know each other before Will comes, is a good idea. But I don't like the idea of Will being on the road in winter. I'm not going to sleep well until he walks in this door."

"The boy has sense, honey. Good sense. He'll be fine."

"Of course he will," Bitty said. "But he might not have a girlfriend by the time he gets here, if you ask me."

"We didn't," Joe muttered, then raised his voice to

add, "Isn't it time that dog of yours had his supper? He's been whinin' at my ankles for an hour."

Jenna laughed. She might miss her husband and worry about her sons, but Joe and Bitty provided enough distractions to keep her smiling. She walked over to the couch and checked on the baby. "I'm ready to be a grandma," she said, turning around to smile at her elderly guests. "I think it's time we go for broke."

Bitty's face lit up. "We could get the flu, all three of us. We'd have to stay in bed upstairs for days and leave them alone down here."

"With Melanie running herself ragged taking care of us?" Joe shook his head. "No way."

"We'll leave them here when we go over to the Rileys' party Saturday night. We'll give them the evening alone." This was from Joe, the old smartie.

"All right." It was risky, Jenna figured, but there wasn't much time to waste. Will should arrive on Sunday, regardless of weather, and Melanie needed time to appreciate her older son's finer qualities.

"Jared won't want to miss the party," Bitty said.

"Leave it to me," Jenna said. "Just go along with whatever I say."

"Well, all right," Uncle Joe drawled. "No one's gonna argue with Grandma."

Jenna grinned. "Damn right."

MELANIE SPENT the next two days telling herself that she was the biggest idiot this side of the Mississippi.

So she did what she always did when she needed to escape reality: she sewed.

Jenna's old Sears Kenmore machine wasn't as modern as the one Melanie owned back home, but it did the job. For two days she pinned and cut and pinned and basted and pinned and sewed until the slipcover was finished, cording and all. The cushions took a little more time and Jenna had to go to town to buy zippers, but they were finished, too. And well before Christmas Day.

Jenna declared her the best houseguest she'd ever had and showed her photos of redecorated kitchens in magazines. And Melanie watched the woman bake an amazing assortment of cookies for Christmas, most of which she hid in strange places so Jared and Uncle Joe wouldn't find them. Aunt Bitty held Beth, fed Fluffy and bossed Joe around. Jared helped hang fresh evergreen branches on the staircase, Jenna lit the lights on the tree every evening and Beth grew accustomed to the room's rocking chair. Melanie fed Beth in the privacy of her bedroom and left messages on her cousin's voice mail. She talked to her aunt, who applauded her niece for making a change and announced she, Uncle Peter and Dylan were going on a last-minute Christmas week cruise.

Melanie supposed she should have worried about Will more, but he called frequently from the road. He never had much to say except to tell them all that he was fine. He sounded more and more frazzled, though, so the driving must not have been easy. She wished she could talk to him privately. She wanted to ask him about his older brother, but for the life of her she didn't know what questions she'd ask. *Does he always have this effect on women?* would be a good one.

"I'll make accent pillows next," Melanie told Jenna. "We'll get stuffing the next time we're in town."

"You're working too hard," she answered. "But I love the results. Do you think I should paint the cupboards white or blue?"

"Cream, I think. To lighten up the room." Melanie lifted Beth from Jenna's arms. The baby yawned and let out a squeak of protest.

"You know, honey, I think Beth might have the sniffles. She seems a little fussy." Jenna patted the baby's back.

"Really?" The baby had never been sick before, but after all that time on the train she might have picked up some germs. Melanie touched her cheek to Beth's forehead. "I can't tell if she feels feverish or not. Can you?"

"I don't think she has a fever," Jenna said. "Tell you what, though. Just to make sure, I'll stay home with her tonight. It's probably not a good idea to take her to a Christmas party."

Joe caught the tail end of the conversation when he and Jared walked into the kitchen. Joe handed Jenna the sewing scissors. "I got 'em nice and sharp now," he said. "What's this about tonight? You're not going to the Rileys' party?"

"You go without me," Jenna said. "You'll have a good time. Matt Casey is going to bring his guitar for singing Christmas carols. And Ida May is bringing her accordion."

Jared, looking very handsome and very cold, gulped. "Her accordion?"

"Yes. She told me she's practiced some new hymns. Just don't forget to take the enchilada casserole I made." She glanced at the clock. "You'd better go get ready. You should leave in about an hour so you don't miss any of the fun."

"I'm staying here," Melanie said. "It's not that I don't appreciate your offer to baby-sit, but it's better that I be here with Beth." She smiled at the older woman. "I'll worry too much if I leave her, even with you."

"Well," Jenna replied. "I can understand that, but I don't want to leave you here all by yourself. What if there's an emergency?"

"I'll stay, Mom." Jared walked over to the counter and poured himself a cup of coffee from the always-on coffeepot. "Joe and Bitty have talked of nothing else but this party for the past couple of days and neither have you."

"Are you sure you don't mind?" Jenna gave him a quick hug. "I do hate to leave Melanie all alone."

"I'll be fine," Melanie hurried to interject. She didn't want to spend the evening alone with the man whose kisses made her all too aware of her erogenous zones. She was a mother now, she reminded herself. Passion was not on her list of things to experience.

But Jenna would not be swayed, and Joe and Bitty

agreed that the Riley Christmas potluck supper was no place for a baby with the sniffles.

"And," Bitty said, "I hear the measles is going around."

Jared's eyebrows rose. "You mean I'm missing out on measles *and* Ida May's music? This must be my lucky night."

"Don't be rude," his mother said. "And keep Melanie company."

Melanie would have rolled her eyes at that statement, except Beth let out a scream that meant she was ready for supper. And by the time Melanie fed her, changed her and returned downstairs, the others had gone and she and Jared were alone. She stood in the entrance to the den and saw that he was stretched out in the recliner, a football game on the television in the corner.

"Before you apologize for forcing me to miss the party," Jared said, holding up his hand as if to ward off her words, "let me tell you that Ida May Casey is tone deaf and her husband, Matt, only knows three chords on the guitar. Which isn't usually tuned, by the way."

She laughed. "So you should be thanking me?"

"Absolutely. Though we're missing out on the enchiladas."

"Your mother made extra. I'll go heat them up, if you're hungry."

He frowned. "You don't have to wait on me."

"Right. Tell me what man doesn't like getting dinner served in front of a football game."

"A *playoff* game." Jared, his hair wet from a very recent shower, looked at the baby. "Is the kid behaving herself?"

Beth, sleepy and content, rested against her hip. "So far. She doesn't seem sick."

"Give the kid to me," he said, surprising her into silence. "We'll watch the Seahawks get their ass kicked while you heat up supper."

Melanie carefully released Beth into Jared's arms. She stopped once to look over her shoulder, just to make sure that Beth was comfortable, and caught Jared looking down at the baby with an unreadable expression in his green eyes. As she fixed dinner, she told herself that it was silly to get so much pleasure from being alone with the rancher. It was too easy to pretend that they were a couple, home with the baby, the leftovers and football on a winter Saturday evening.

He brought the cradle downstairs so they could eat in the den. They drank cold beer and ate chips with hot salsa and cheered Denver to a one-point lead over the Seahawks. Beth, sneeze-free and content, slept in the cradle despite the noise. Melanie suspected her daughter preferred to be in the middle of things whenever possible.

"Okay," Jared said, clearing the coffee table of dishes. "Where are they?"

"Where are what?" She took one last swallow of beer. She'd read somewhere that beer was good for nursing mothers, but she didn't share that fact with Jared, of course.

He leaned over her, his hands on both arms of the chair. "You know. Shaped like candy canes. Taste like peppermint. Red sugar frosting. Ring a bell?"

Melanie laughed. "I can't tell you."

"She'll never know."

"Your mother counts the cookies as she puts them in the boxes."

His face was very close and his grin made him look younger. And sexier. And very, very appealing. She must have a weakness for dark-haired men, Melanie realized. Or maybe it was the cowboy boots or the way his eyes crinkled at the corners when he teased.

"But you know where they are." He hesitated, his smile fading as he looked down at her. He was thinking about kissing her and she was thinking about how much she would like that. She wondered if he knew how much.

"I do, but I can't tell," she whispered, her throat dry as he lowered his mouth to hers. "This isn't fair."

His lips touched hers softly, then lifted to trail along her jaw and lower, to the small hollow behind her earlobe. "What's not fair?"

"You're trying to weaken my resistance so I'll tell you where the cookies are."

"What cookies?" He found her mouth again, kissing her with a deliberate slowness that began an ache between her thighs. It wasn't fair that he should be able to affect her that way, and yet, feeling alive again was exhilarating. She was so tired of being sad.

She wanted to reach up and pull him closer, so she did. He slipped beside her on the couch, pulled her into his lap and never broke the kiss. It was as if he couldn't get enough of her any more than she could resist him. He skimmed his hands underneath her sweater and sent her skin tingling. He palmed her sides, slid his thumbs close to the sensitive peaks of her breasts.

"Jared," she managed to say, when his mouth left hers to tickle her ear. She thought she heard ringing and prayed she didn't. He was an excellent kisser, capable of making her think of nothing but making love. He stilled and she pulled away to look at him. She was nestled in his lap and was aware that she was not the only one aroused to the point of doing something foolish. His hands, moving across her breasts, stilled.

"The phone," she whispered, her voice shaky.

He muttered something under his breath.

"It could be your family," she insisted. "If no one answers they'll think something is wrong."

Another ring turned on the answering machine, but Beth woke up and began to cry as if her heart was breaking.

"Hell," Jared said, cupping her waist and lifting her off his lap. "It's probably for the best."

For the best? What on earth did he mean by that? Melanie hurried to the center of the room and picked Beth up. She stopped crying almost immediately and nestled into her mother's neck. She would pretend it never happened, that her knees weren't weak and her heart wasn't pounding as if she'd run up three flights of stairs.

"They're under your mother's bed," Melanie said, watching as Jared went into the kitchen and pushed the button to hear the latest telephone message. "In a pink plastic sweater box."

"What are you talking about?" Every inch the grumpy, frustrated male, Jared walked back into the den, the portable phone up to his ear. "It was a *telemarketer*, for cripe's sake."

"The cookies. And besides, you said it was for the best," she repeated, straightening her sweater with her free hand.

"I lied." He tossed the phone into the recliner and eyed Beth. "It's late," he said.

"Yes. We're going to bed."

"Good idea." But the expression on his face was anything but encouraging. She wanted to go into his arms, for only one minute more, but it was best they not start that up again. For some reason the physical attraction between them was strong, undeniable and terribly tempting.

He followed her upstairs with the cradle, but didn't linger in the bedroom.

Thank goodness.

6

"DO YOU BELIEVE IN LOVE at first sight?" was probably the dumbest question he'd ever asked anyone. And on the Saturday night before Christmas, on the twenty-first of December, Jared swore into the receiver after reaching his brother's voice mail. Where in hell was Will? He didn't like this crazy idea his brother had of driving home. Storms came up fast and the interstate got shut down all the time. The wind caused drifts a semi didn't dare drive through.

He was damn sure he was going to stay up all night and wait for Will's call if he had to, because he was going to talk to his brother and find out once and for all what was the deal with Melanie Briggs. He'd almost made love to her, for Pete's sake. If the phone hadn't rung, that's exactly what would have happened. They'd been pretty hot and heavy on the old sofa, like two teenagers who'd finally gotten a chance to be alone.

He'd been glad to skip the Rileys' party. He wasn't antisocial or anything, but Mrs. Riley was never too subtle when it came to trying to fix up her daughter—home from Denver every holiday—with him. They'd had a thing going in high school and had been friends ever since, but her mother never gave up hope. Jared dated occasionally now, though there weren't too many single women between here and Great Falls, and no one had come close to intriguing him the way Melanie did.

No, he was a goner from the moment Melanie smiled at him in the train station. And tonight he'd even held the baby. She'd curled her little pink fingers around his rough thumb and looked up at him with those big blue eyes as if she wanted to ask him who he was.

Not Daddy, that's for sure. He might have fallen hard for the houseguest, but people didn't make up their minds about the rest of their lives after knowing someone for six—no, five—days.

Especially not a cautious man like himself.

The phone rang and Jared grabbed it before it rang again. When he heard his brother laughing, he cursed and told him everything.

"I'M SORRY YOU MISSED the party," Jenna said, drying the last of the dishes. "Beth seems fine this morning. Did she sleep well last night?"

"She only woke me up once," Melanie said. "She ate and went right back to sleep."

"What a good girl," Jenna said, walking over to where the baby snuggled in her car seat on the couch. "Mommy must be very happy with you," she cooed.

Yes, Melanie wanted to say, but it had more to do with Jared's kisses than Beth's sleep habits. Feeling happy again was a strange experience. And even though there was no guarantee that such a feeling would last, Melanie found herself humming Christmas carols as she stuffed the last of the decorative pillows for Jenna's kitchen sofa. Fluffy sat beside the baby and watched her with great fascination every time Beth kicked her feet. Every once in a while Melanie stopped working in order to replace tiny white socks over tiny pink feet.

"Fluffy!" Bitty tapped her cane on the kitchen floor. "Time to go out!"

The little dog lay down and put his head on his paws and Melanie smiled. Poor Fluffy was smitten with the baby, following Beth from place to place and only leaving the baby's side when it was time to eat or Beth went to sleep upstairs.

"Darn that dog," Bitty fumed, stomping over to the couch. "He doesn't mind any better than anyone else around here. Well, those pillows sure look nice, dear."

"Thank you." She tucked one blue-and-tan-striped pillow in the corner of the sofa. "There. What do you think?"

"Nice color," Bitty said, leaning on her cane. "Jenna, we should keep this young woman in Montana. There hasn't been a seamstress in the family in three generations."

"Bitty, for heaven's sake," Jenna said, coming over

to look at the newly covered sofa and matching pillows. "Very nice, Melanie. This is turning out to be a wonderful Christmas." She smiled, but Melanie saw that the woman's expression was worried. "If only Will would get here—"

"Give him a call." Melanie scratched Fluffy's ears. "Find out what state he's in now. Maybe he's closer than you think." And maybe, after he arrived, he could help her figure out his brother. Or maybe not. Explaining her sudden attraction to Jared—in a strictly sexual way, of course—was not something to discuss with another man. She certainly couldn't ask Bitty or Jenna, and Dylan was on a Christmas cruise somewhere in the Bahamas.

"He'll call when he can, I'm sure. Or maybe he'll just walk through the door to surprise me," Jenna said, smoothing one hand over the new fabric. "Has anyone seen Jared this afternoon?"

"He and Joe went into town," Bitty said. "I promised that old man I'd play cards with him tonight."

"Christmas Eve is soon," Jenna said, glancing toward the kitchen window. "Will has never missed Christmas Eve before. He should have taken the train with you instead of waiting to get his work done."

Melanie didn't think that traveling with an infant would be Will's first choice of transportation.

Beth began to fuss, but it was Jenna who lifted her into her arms for comfort. Melanie leaned back against the couch and watched her daughter smile at

Jared's mother. "Do you want to see the pretty tree lights again? I'll bet you do, sweetheart, don't you?"

Fluffy jumped off the couch to hover at Jenna's ankles, but Bitty scooped him up. "It's wee-wee time for you," she said, taking him to the back door.

Melanie followed Jenna into the living room, now festive in evergreen bows, red gingham bows and fat ivory candles. The tree stood in the corner, lavishly decorated with ornaments that had been in the Stone family for many generations. Jenna hit the switch that turned the lights on, then stood near the tree so Beth could see the sparkly decorations. But it was to Melanie she spoke.

"Do you like Montana, Melanie? Do you like the ranch?"

"Yes," she said. "From what I've seen, very much."

"And your life in Washington? What is that like?"

Melanie reached over and adjusted an ornament that was hanging too close to the end of a branch. Jenna wasn't making small talk. And Melanie suspected the purpose of the questions. "It's very quiet," she said. "I work with my cousin in her design business and I take Beth with me wherever I go."

"I've always thought that when my sons married, I would move nearby to the old foreman's house. It's a lovely place, but it needs some work. I've seen a lot of things on the decorating shows I'd like to try."

"But this is your home."

"It's a big house to take care of," Jenna replied.

"And it needs a younger woman to do it." The baby put her palm on Jenna's chin and chuckled. "There are lots of rooms for babies upstairs."

"Jenna—" She wanted to explain that she was not going to stay here past next week, that she wasn't going to marry Will and live in Jenna's house, but the older woman interrupted her.

"Forgive me the question," she said, "but are you in love with my son?"

"Will and I are j-just friends," Melanie stammered. "I've said that before."

Jenna didn't take her gaze from Melanie's face, not even when Beth let out an earsplitting screech. "And if I said I wasn't asking about Will?"

She took a deep breath and tried to forget the way Jared's fingers felt against her skin. Was she falling in love or just desperate to be held? "Then I wouldn't know how to answer that. Jared is...different."

"He's a good man."

"Yes."

"He's not as easy to know as Will. But his feelings run deep. Too deep, sometimes," she admitted with a wry smile. "But that doesn't mean he's unfeeling and cold."

"No." *Cold* would not describe the man who almost made love to her last night. "Not cold at all."

SHE WAS FREEZING. She was also thirsty, ravenous and wide awake, despite the fact that it was three-fourteen on Tuesday morning and now officially Christmas Eve. Melanine tiptoed down the stairs, through the dark hall, past the den and the living room, until she reached the kitchen. Jenna always left a small light on, just in case someone needed a snack in the middle of the night. Melanie suspected Jared's mother also left a plate of cookies on the counter for Joe to feast on before he went upstairs to bed.

Sure enough, a plastic box of cookies sat on the counter, with a note that read "Okay to eat" in Jenna's neat handwriting. She poured herself a large glass of milk, picked four fat sugar cookies from the container, grabbed a napkin from the holder and tiptoed into the den. The next time she went to Duggan she was going to buy slippers, the fat, fuzzy kind with fleece lining.

And if she knew anything about fires, she would poke at the embers still burning in the den fireplace and add a log, but she didn't dare. She sat on the floor, her knees drawn up under her gown, as close to the fireplace as possible. If she had been a Girl Scout instead of playing with Aunt Lilian's sewing machine to make doll clothes, she'd know how to get warm.

"Hey," a voice behind her said. "You're not going to share?"

She turned and almost knocked over her milk. Jared got up from the recliner and walked toward her. "Don't scare me like that."

"Sorry." He smiled. Or at least she thought he did. The light was too poor to be certain. "You're sneaking cookies, too?"

"It's not sneaking when there's a sign that reads 'Okay,'" she pointed out, unable to help smiling at him. His dark hair was rumpled, his shirt half-buttoned and hanging over his jeans. He looked handsome and accessible, not the imposing rancher who'd been avoiding her. She fidgeted a little, took a bite of cookie. She'd been foolish not to pack a robe, even though it would have taken up too much room. Her long flannel nightgown was nothing to be embarrassed about, and she wore her favorite oversize cardigan for warmth, but she still felt exposed. "What are you doing up so late?"

"Same thing as you," he said. "I couldn't sleep and I thought I heard Joe in the kitchen, so I got up to keep him company." He added two logs to the embers, then used the poker to coax a flame. Within minutes the fire erupted into a small blaze. He sat down beside her on the rug, and when she scooted over to give him room, her bare foot touched his hand.

"Good God, woman, your feet are like ice."

"The fire will—" She stopped talking the minute he took her foot into his hands and began to rub it.

"Don't you have any socks?" He spoke in a rough voice, irritated at her idiocy, but he rubbed warmth into her skin with his callused hands.

Since a lot more of her body was heating up besides

her toes, Melanie didn't have a ready answer for the question. When Jared reached for her other foot she moved her milk and cookies so she could lean back on her arms and let him work his magic on the other foot. He drew her feet across his thigh.

"I have socks," she said, though she wanted to close her eyes and simply enjoy the sensation. "Upstairs in my suitcase."

"Better?" He stopped rubbing.

"Yes. Much." She opened her eyes, but Jared didn't release her feet. His fingers curved around her ankles, as if testing their circumference.

"You'd wear a small pair of boots," he said.

She was suddenly very glad she'd taken the time to shave her legs this morning. If she flexed her foot against his thigh she wondered if she would touch more than his leg. It was tempting to find out, but she knew she would be playing with fire. Anyone in the family could wake up and come downstairs, and besides, she had no business wondering what making love to Jared would be like. Hot, she thought. Slow and strong and all-consuming.

"I should probably finish my cookies and go back to bed." She should probably stay there from now on and not wander around at night as if she lived alone.

"But I built a fire for you." His smile was slow, his hands still holding her legs.

"I'm warm enough now." To show how casual she felt about all of this foot-warming business, Melanie reached for her milk, intending to take a sip. Instead she miscalculated and knocked it over. "Oh, shoot!"

"Here." Jared let go of her legs and took off his shirt. He tossed it on top of the puddle that was seeping across the wood floor to the edge of the rug. "Use that."

"Thanks." The cotton was warm from his skin, but she concentrated on cleaning up the mess. She took the shirt to the kitchen and rinsed it under the faucet while Jared grabbed a roll of paper towels and finished cleaning the floor.

"Leave it," he said when he saw her ringing the water from his shirt. "I'll throw it in the laundry in the morning."

"Okay." She turned to see that he was naked from the waist up. He had a magnificent chest, wide and muscled, with a triangle of hair in its center and trailing low, to disappear behind the waistband of his jeans. "Well," she said, forcing her gaze upward to the area around his chin. "I guess I'd better go back to bed."

"Yes," he said, looking down at her as if she wore a sexy, black, see-through gown. "I guess you should."

And neither one of them moved.

Of course, she thought later, she should have known what was going to happen the minute she discovered she wasn't alone in the den. She should have gotten up, excused herself and taken her snack to her bedroom. That would have been the best way to avoid temptation. And spilled milk.

Instead she'd practically fallen against his naked chest when he'd kissed her. Her palms were flat against all that male heat and his arms encircled her, held her tightly against his body. And that was where Melanie wanted to be, held tight against his skin. She hadn't been touched in so long, hadn't been desired or felt desirable. She'd been grieving, in shock and big as a hippo while pregnant, and since Beth's arrival, the thought of making love to someone seemed as foreign as dancing in a topless bar. And about as appealing.

Until Jared.

Until he kissed her as she'd never been kissed before, with an amazing passion and need, as if she was the most desirable woman in all of Montana. Maybe she should have been a little stronger, she thought later. Maybe she should have ended it right there and then. But she hadn't.

She'd kissed him until she couldn't breathe, kissed him while his hands roved along her body, over her breasts and along the curve of her spine. His large hands cupped her buttocks and pulled her tighter against him. Her hands skimmed his chest, tickled his chest hair, reached for his shoulders. His fingers drew the flannel nightgown higher.

"We can't—"

"We can," he murmured.

"Not here," Melanie managed to say. Her lips touched his breastbone; she heard the rapid beat of his heart.

"The den, then."

"Someone could come downstairs." She looked up at him to see him frown.

"I guess you'll just have to come upstairs to my bed," he said, his voice low. He grimaced when she shook her head.

"Beth could cry and I wouldn't hear her."

Jared didn't seem deterred by that objection. He gripped her waist and lifted her off her feet as if she weighed less than her daughter. "Hang on," he said, tipping her over his shoulder.

"What are you doing?" She wriggled and attempted to get down, but he was already heading to the hall.

"Shh. If anyone is still awake—which I doubt, by the way—they'll only hear one set of footsteps."

"This is just like in the movies," she whispered, conscious of his arm around the back of her thighs. At least her nightgown was still covering most of her.

"Shh," he said again. "And hold on."

"Where are we going?"

He didn't answer her, because by that time they were at the stairs. True to his word, Jared moved quietly from tread to tread, barely making a sound. Melanie held her breath for fear Uncle Joe or Bitty's door would open and they would demand an explanation for Jared hauling her upstairs like a sack of potatoes.

I hurt my ankle, she could say. *I twisted my knee. I know it looks like your nephew is carrying me upstairs to bed to make wild and passionate love, but any contact between us is strictly for reasons of first aid. Really.*

But no one appeared in the dim glow of the hall night-light, and Jared opened the door to Melanie's room without making a sound. Once inside, he set her on her feet and closed the door behind him. She checked on Beth, whose breathing was deep and even, before turning around to face the man who brought her up to bed.

"You can change your mind," he said, his voice so low she could barely hear his words. "But I hope like hell you don't."

"Shh." She reached for his hand and led him close to her unmade bed. The quilts had been thrown back, exposing cotton sheets covered with tiny yellow tulips. It looked very inviting and very...final. "I'm nervous," she confessed.

"Me, too." His big hands began to undo the row of buttons that ran from the gown's collar to waist. "I've wanted to touch you since the first moment I saw you at the train station."

The buttons open, he slid the nightgown—and her sweater—past her shoulders and down her arms. The clothes fell to the floor and Melanie shivered as the cool air touched her skin, but she wasn't embarrassed about her nakedness. He looked at her as if she was beautiful, as if he could look at her for hours and still be entranced. And then he kissed her, opening her mouth and teasing her tongue with his while her breasts were warm against his chest.

"Give me a minute to get something," he said, finally lifting his head. "I'll be right back."

"What—oh." He left the room as silently as he'd entered as Melanie realized he was going to get a condom. She should have thought of that herself, especially since her gynecologist had warned her that nursing mothers could still get pregnant. She had laughed at that, thinking that making love was as about as remote as going on a date. Neither one had been in her future and yet here she was, sliding under the covers of her bed, waiting for a rancher named Jared Stone to join her.

She should have been shocked at herself, but she could think of nothing else she wanted to do more than to be held by this man. And when he returned to the room he smiled at her and dropped the condom packets on the nightstand. He unzipped his jeans and slid them—along with his navy boxer shorts—down his legs and kicked them off. She'd made room in the bed for him, but when he slid underneath the covers she was still surprised with herself for enjoying the length of male flesh suddenly against her. She'd missed this. She was on her side, and he faced her, smoothing the hair from her face and kissing her gently.

His lips found her ear to whisper, "Have you made love since you had Beth?"

She shook her head no.

He drew back to look into her eyes. "I don't want to hurt you," he whispered.

"You won't," she said, though she wasn't entirely sure.

"We'll go slow?"

"Yes." *Slow* was good. *Slow* would give her time to accustom herself to this man and his body, to the strange experience of having a man in her bed again, time to remember passion and forget grief. It was only for this once, she thought. There wouldn't be another night like this, a time when they were alone and everyone else was asleep. Christmas was almost here and Will would arrive before it.

Jared's hand slid along her hip and pulled her closer to him. She felt his erection, hot and hard against her inner thigh. Her own reaction was a melting need that caught her breath in her throat. He tipped his head to kiss her, soothing her mouth, while his hand swept over her thigh. He was letting her feel him, giving her time to adjust to their nakedness under the cool sheets, but Melanie didn't want time. She wanted him. Her hand rubbed his chest, curiously dared to go lower. His fingers found her, moving slowly between her thighs to slide easily along the wetness there. She was ready for him, but he didn't hurry.

Maybe, she thought, trying not to climax against his fingers, he also knows that this isn't going to happen again. She moved closer, ran her fingertips around the head of his penis, heard him moan into her mouth. He left her for a moment and then returned to the heated spot in the bed. His mouth returned to hers, his fingers stroked her abdomen and lower, teasing and caressing until she knew she had to have more.

She had to have *him*. When she reached for him, he tipped her onto her back and gently moved over her, spread her thighs wide.

"If I hurt you—"

"You won't," she promised, reveling in having him between her legs. With one smooth, slow movement he entered her and paused to look into her eyes to see that she was okay. Melanie urged him deeper. She wanted to be full of him, needed to have him deep inside so that she felt whole again. She felt greedy and hot, her sensitized skin brushing his with every move he made.

He took his time, as if he was memorizing the feel of her with every stroke. And with each stroke he went deeper, until she thought she would die from the pleasure he gave her. She was careful to be quiet, conscious of the loud rustle of the sheets and the whispered words of approval Jared brushed against her throat. She urged him higher and faster, until she surrendered completely to the whirling heat that centered deep within her. He caught her mouth with his when she climaxed, captured the sounds she made to protect their secret.

And when his own climax followed hers, Melanie held back tears and kept him deep inside her until his breathing settled.

"Stay?" she asked moments later when he moved off of her. He paused, then lay on his side facing her and pulled the covers up to cover them.

"For a while," he promised. "I'll leave before anyone else wakes up."

She was suddenly exhausted, so she turned on her side away from him but stayed in the comforting circle of his arms. He tucked her bottom firmly against him and she heard his soft chuckle as her cold toes touched his shins and quickly moved away.

"Sorry," she whispered. "I guess my feet are still cold."

"I'll warm them." He wrapped his leg over hers and pulled her feet back where they were, tucked in between his calves.

"How can you stand it?"

"It must be love," Jared said, his chin resting atop her head.

Oh, no, she thought, a chill sliding over her heart. Not love.

"YOU'RE LOOKING FULL of Christmas spirit this morning." Uncle Joe leaned against the stall boards and watched Jared check the condition of one of the mares.

"It's Christmas Eve, isn't it?" Jared patted the bay's neck. He'd had to find work to do in the barn this morning in order to stop himself from creeping back into Melanie's room. Not to make love to her, necessarily, but just to look at her. Just to make sure she was okay.

"Yeah, I know what day it is. That brother of yours better get here soon or your mother is gonna wear herself out going to the window."

"He said he'd be home today the last time I talked to him." He owed a great deal to the telephone. Being able to talk to Will had enabled him to kiss Melanie without guilt and even better, to be able to make love to her without feeling as if he were committing an act of treason.

"Did you ask him about Melanie and what was goin' on?"

"Yeah. They're just friends." He looked up and grinned at Joe. "Just friends."

"Yeah, I thought as much," the old man said. "I think he was more interested in finding a gal for you than he was for himself."

Jared didn't answer. He was busy remembering how good he'd felt enclosed in Melanie's body, how she'd gasped when he pleased her.

"You coming in for breakfast?"

"Yeah." He cleared his throat and tried to look casual. Damn right he was coming in for breakfast. He hadn't seen Melanie since he'd slipped from her room this morning. Beth had started crying, which woke them both up, and he'd scooped up the baby and given her to her mother before leaving for his own room. There'd been no one in the hall, which hadn't been a surprise. But from the way Joe was looking at him, Jared wondered if the old man suspected something.

Well, it didn't matter. Because if everything went the way he wanted it to, he wouldn't have secrets to hide much longer.

THE FIRST THING MELANIE wanted to do was pack. But the ranch wasn't a place where she could call for a taxi to drive her to the train station, which was hours away. And her timing couldn't have been worse, since it was the morning of Christmas Eve. She was a guest on a remote ranch and was expected to share in the holiday festivities. And not sleep with one of the hosts, either. And certainly not fall in love—if it was love—with one of them.

The second thing she wanted to do was cry, but since Beth was already doing enough of that for both of them, joining in would only give her a headache. Besides, Jenna would question her red-rimmed eyes and there was no way Melanie could say, "I feel awful about having sex with your son a few hours ago."

Having sex. Making love. Whatever Melanie called it in her head, the overriding reason for such behavior was still the same: she'd fallen in love with the man.

Or even worse, she was simply being weak and needy and ready for a strong pair of arms to hold her for a few hours. She didn't know which was worse, but when it came time to take the weeping baby and go downstairs for breakfast, Melanie knew that somehow she had to get out of town, even before Will—whose good deeds had gotten her into this mess—arrived to celebrate Christmas with his family.

Even if she could convince Will to take her to a bus stop in Duggan, this was Beth's first Christmas and shouldn't be spent in some truck stop. Melanie wanted to put her daughter's gifts under the tree and tell her that Santa had left them for her, even if Beth was too young to understand. She wanted pictures for Beth's baby album, wanted to sing "Silent Night" with the Stones when they went to church tomorrow. She wanted to eat cookies and turkey and cranberry cake.

She wanted to run far, far away.

Melanie held her daughter and patted her back until Beth hiccupped and fell asleep. She lay her down into the cradle and then rocked it gently until she was certain Beth was asleep. She would take a quick shower, she would pack up her things and then she would come up with a way to leave the ranch without hurting anyone's feelings, without crying and without kissing Jared goodbye.

None of that sounded possible.

"TAKE MELANIE SOME COFFEE," Jenna said, stopping Jared as soon as he'd hung up his coat and replaced his wet boots with a pair of moccasins. "I heard her with the baby, but she hasn't come down for breakfast yet."

"Sure." Jared took the mug his mother handed him. He was heading upstairs, anyway. He'd messed around outside for as long as he could stand it, but some things couldn't wait. Like seeing the woman he loved. Getting to know that baby of hers. Seeing her shy smile when he kissed her good morning.

He hurried upstairs as fast as he could without spilling the coffee, then knocked quietly on the door, just in case Beth was asleep. "Melanie? It's me. I brought—"

When she opened the door he could tell right away that she'd been crying. Beth sobbed and hiccupped, signaling the end of an unhappy session.

"Hey," he said, feeling a pain in his gut at the thought of Melanie's tears. "What's wrong?"

"I think—" she paused, swallowed hard "—I'd better go."

"Go?" He stepped inside the room and shut the door behind him. Without thinking, he set the mug on the dresser and lifted the baby from Melanie's arms. Beth didn't seem to mind. A soggy, warm bundle, she lay against his chest and sighed. "Go where, sweetheart?"

"That's the problem," Melanie replied, reaching for a tissue from her opened tote bag. "I don't know."

And then he saw the suitcase, open and half-packed on the bed. His gaze returned to Melanie, who was dressed in blue jeans and the brown sweater she'd worn when he'd first seen her. He couldn't bear the thought of losing her, but he couldn't stand to see her so unhappy. He had to ask. "Because of last night?"

"Partly."

"And what else?" He sat on the edge of the bed and ignored the suitcase next to him.

"I can't...care for you, Jared." Her gaze dropped to her child, snuggled in his arms and now, he suspected, asleep. So it all came back to Beth's father. And it was sure as hell time for that particular mystery to be solved.

"Tell me about him," he said.

She didn't have to ask who he meant. "Everything?"

"Whatever you want to tell me. And especially whatever you don't want to tell me."

"I loved him."

"Okay." Jealousy, sharp and painful, pierced his gut, but he kept his expression blank.

"We grew up together, went to high school and
college and never dated anyone else. We were going
to get married." She hesitated, leaving Jared to wonder if the man was crazy to have gone off and left her.
"I'd just found out I was pregnant and then he died.
In a plane crash."

"September 11?"

Melanie shook her head. "No. It was one of those
small private planes. He was going to a meeting in
Kansas City and the engines quit. He and the pilot
were killed."

"I'm sorry." Which was the truth. He couldn't bear
to see the pain in her eyes.

"Yes. I know. That's the problem."

"What?"

"You feel sorry for me. Everyone does. Which is
why I couldn't bear to spend Christmas at home."

"You think all of this—" He stopped and took a
deep breath before he continued. "You think I made
love to you because I felt sorry for you?"

"Not exactly, but—"

"You think I want to marry you out of pity?"

Her eyes were huge. "*Marry* you?"

"Saturday night I called Will and asked him how
he felt about you. When he stopped laughing he told
me he'd figured we'd be perfect for each other. He
wasn't feeling sorry for you when he asked you to the
ranch—he was fixing you up with his older brother."

Jared stood and carefully placed the baby into the

cradle. He covered her up with the horse-print blanket before he turned back to Melanie. Then he reached into his shirt pocket and pulled out a small red package. A flattened crimson bow covered the top of the box.

"Here," he said, dropping it onto the jumble of clothes on the bed. "You can take it or leave it. I love you, of course. I was pretty much done for the minute I saw you. I'd be a good father to Beth and I'd do just about anything in the world to make you happy. But I sure as hell won't keep you from leaving if you don't love me."

"It's not as simple as falling in love with you," Melanie said. "I wish it was, but it's not."

"Yes, it is," he replied. "If you're still in love with Beth's father, okay, I can accept that. If you need time, I can understand that, too. But running away? I thought you had more guts than that. You could at least stick around and find out if what we've got is worth taking hold of."

Jared waited for her to say something, but she was silent. Well, that was all right, too. Better than hearing her say she was leaving. He turned and opened the door, but before he left he added, "Just let me know when you're ready. I'll take you anywhere you want to go."

"LOOK." JOE POINTED OUT the kitchen window. "A car's comin' up the road. I'll bet I know who that is."

Jenna and Bitty hurried from the kitchen table to see for themselves, while Fluffy stayed under the table to finish his cinnamon toast.

"That had better be Will," Jenna declared. "He promised—oh, look. He's flashing his lights on and off. That's Will, all right."

"It's about time," Bitty said, wiping her eyes with a tissue. "He sure cut it close, though."

Melanie, Beth against her shoulder, hesitated in the doorway. She'd be glad to see Will at last, but he was not the brother she needed to talk to at the moment. She met Jared's questioning gaze and tried to smile.

"Are you ready?" he said, his mouth a grim line.

"Yes." Her voice was a little wobbly, so she tried again. "*Yes.*"

"Now?"

"Well," she said. "Maybe not now. Don't we have to get a license and blood tests?"

He stood very still, so still she wondered if he was breathing. "What did you say?"

"I said, don't we have to get a license and—" She stopped, unsure of the expression in his eyes. "Jared?"

He was in front of her in three strides. His callused hands framed her face as he looked down at her. "Melanie? What made you change your mind?"

"I'm not a coward," she answered. "Not really. After you left I tried to keep packing, but the more I tried to pack the less it made sense to leave you. I fell in love with you and it scared me half to death."

"And now?" His voice was a whisper, as if by asking he dared hope.

"I'm still scared, but I do know how much I love you. And what kind of example would I set for my daughter if I ran away from love?"

"Good point," he said, finally daring to smile. He kissed her softly, careful not to bump the baby. She raised her left hand to his as he tilted her face. "I should propose to you again. Do it right this time."

She wanted to laugh, she wanted to cry, she wanted this feeling of lightness to go on forever. "In front of your mother, Joe and Bitty?"

He grimaced. "Maybe not." Fluffy whined at Melanie's feet, then barked his displeasure at not being closer to the baby. "Maybe we'd better find a nice quiet place in the barn where I can show you—"

"Jared!"

They turned to see three pairs of eyes staring at them. Jared dropped his hands, but put one arm around Melanie's shoulders as if he'd been doing it for years.

"Congratulate me," he said. "We're getting married."

Joe's mouth dropped open and Aunt Bitty gasped, "For heaven's sake!"

"No," Melanie said, as the sight of Jenna's tears made her own tears threaten to spill over. "For Christmas."

I'LL BE HOME
FOR CHRISTMAS

1

Tuesday, December 17
Washington, D.C.

"WHAT HAVE YOU DONE WITH HER?"

Will Stone eyed the beautiful young woman standing in the corridor in front of his apartment and wondered if he'd ever seen her before. No, he would have remembered anyone in the office of the Crop Protection Association who looked like Cameron Diaz and Heather Locklear rolled into one. "What have I done with who? I mean, whom?"

She attempted to peer past him into the apartment. "My cousin."

"I think you have the wrong apartment." Ordinarily he would appreciate such unexpected company, but not this morning. This morning he was in a bind, having overslept.

"I'm sure I don't. The doorman told me this was the right one. He said you would know where my cousin is."

"Look," Will said. "I don't have time for games." He was already running late. Very late. "I'm really busy. I've got a flight to catch this morning and I'm not finished packing.''

"You're not even dressed."

"It's not even eight o'clock," he pointed out. "I wasn't expecting company." He certainly wasn't expecting a streaky-blond-haired dynamo with big blue eyes and a body that would tempt a monk. His gaze swept over her red sweater, black leather jacket and matching short skirt. All expensive, he'd bet. He ran one hand through his uncombed hair. "You're lucky I'm wearing anything at all."

One beautifully shaped eyebrow rose as she looked at his naked chest, then up to his face. "And you're lucky I haven't called the police."

"The police." He wished he'd had a cup of coffee before opening the door to this insane person. Maybe he'd have more patience—or find more humor in the situation. He definitely would have to quit making jokes, because this woman didn't think he was funny. "Why on earth would you want to call the police?"

"I told you," she said, revealing an impatience that made him take a step backward. "I'm looking for my cousin and I want to know what you did with her."

"Okay. I'll play along. Who's your cousin?"

"Melanie," she said, her voice getting loud. "Melanie Briggs. Ring a bell?"

"Hey, keep it down." He opened the door wider and let the gorgeous maniac into his living room. "I know where Melanie is. Why didn't you tell me her name in the first place?"

The woman looked around the room as if she expected Melanie to be hiding behind the nine-foot ivory chenille sofa. "She left me a note and said she was going to spend Christmas at a ranch with Will Stone, a man she met in her apartment building. Are you Will Stone?"

"Yes," he said, though admitting it was only going to cost him precious time.

"So where is she?"

"She's in—wait a minute. Melanie said she didn't want to spend the holidays with her family." Will went over to his suitcase, spread open on the glass coffee table, and pulled out a clean T-shirt. "Now, if you'll excuse me, I've got to get in the shower."

The woman, who bore little resemblance to her mild-mannered, brown-haired cousin, sat on the couch as if she was going to spend the rest of her life there. She crossed a pair of long, lean legs and dangled a red high heel from her left foot. Elegant fingers hooked a section of blond hair behind her ear, revealing dangling earrings that looked like tiny red Christmas ornaments. All in all, she was an amazing picture of composure and sexiness at such an early hour. He assumed she was on her way to work, but he'd bet his truck that she didn't work on Capitol Hill.

"So," he tried again, "now that we've cleared that up, you can be on your way."

"Not so fast, cowboy." She rummaged through a large purse and pulled out a cell phone.

"I'm not a cowboy," he said. "I'm a rancher. There's a difference."

She shrugged, her concentration on pushing buttons on the tiny phone. She held it up to her ear and waited, then frowned. "She's not answering her phone. I bought her the thing for her birthday and she won't use it."

Will smiled. Melanie wasn't much for cell phones. His neighbor preferred conversations in the elevator and never seemed to mind when he walked along beside her for a while when she took the baby out in her carriage. Melanie lacked the sophistication of this blond cousin, but her friendship had become important to him.

"So?"

He looked at her. "So?"

"Where is she?"

Will decided the only way to get rid of her was to tell her the truth. "She's in Montana."

"She can't be." The blond beauty looked as if she was going to burst into tears. He really hoped she wouldn't. In his experience with women, tears always took up a great deal of time. And time was something he didn't have, not if he was going to go home today.

"She is," he declared, moving toward the door. He held it open and made a waving motion with his T-shirt, hoping she'd get the idea. "Safe and sound in the bosom of my family."

"But she wouldn't fly to Montana."

"No," he said, knowing full well the reason Melanie wouldn't get on a plane, even a large passenger jet. "She took the train."

"The *train?* With the *baby?*"

"Yeah. She said it would give her time to think. And time to see the country." He glanced at his watch. Cripe, with traffic and the new airport regulations, he'd be lucky to make his flight. And he still had to pick up Doris. "Look, Melanie is fine, Beth is fine, they left D.C. last Saturday and they arrived in Havre—"

"Havre?" She frowned as if she'd repeated an X-rated word.

"Montana," he answered. "They got there yesterday afternoon and now are sleeping peacefully at the ranch."

"Says you."

"Says the message on my voice mail," he answered. "Who *are* you?"

"Dylan Briggs," she replied, lifting her stubborn chin as if she dared him to argue with her. "I'm Mel's best friend and cousin. I just returned from France last night and found the note she left me. I can't believe she just took off like that."

He held the door open wider. "Well, she did. Now, out you go."

She looked at his open suitcase and lifted his plane tickets from the table. She studied them for a moment before she dropped them back where they were. "How long have you lived here?"

"I sublet the place for three months," he answered. "Melanie lives next door."

"Yes," she said, fixing her shoe onto her right foot before she stood. "I know."

"Thanks for dropping by." If this was a normal day, he would have made coffee and offered her a cup. He would have teased a smile out of her, made her laugh, asked her out to dinner. He would have taken a few more long looks at her legs, too. But Doris and Northwest Airlines were waiting for him.

Dylan Briggs walked slowly—very slowly—to the door. "If you've hurt my cousin in any way—" She stopped and looked up at him. "Believe me, you'll never get away with it."

"I think you watch too much television," he said with a sigh, before shutting the door behind her.

OKAY, SHE COULD HAVE BEEN nicer to the man. She could have ignored the jet lag, the painful way her panty hose bit into her waist, the blister on her heel. She could have—should have—turned on the charm and discovered exactly where Mel and Beth were and why. None of this made any sense. Dylan took the elevator down to the lobby and hurried outside to call a cab. She could have just as easily taken the subway, but she couldn't afford to waste a minute. Call her crazy, call her overprotective, call her a teeny bit paranoid, Dylan didn't care.

She'd been taking care of Mel since the six-year-old orphan came to her house to live after her parents died. Two years older and wiser, Dylan had shared Barbie dolls, books, friends and a bedroom with the girl who was closer to her than any sister could be. Why Mel had decided to spend Christmas with Beth in Montana—*Montana*, of all places—made absolutely no sense.

And Dylan was determined to find out exactly what was going on. Now that she'd seen this Stone guy, Dylan found it less difficult to blame her cousin for deserting the family at Christmas. If anything could pull Mel out of her depression—grief-induced, postpartum depression—it would be the sight of a half-naked cowboy. *That* half-naked cowboy.

Oh, he could use some help in the charm department. And his apartment, sublet or not, screamed "dull." But the dimple in his left cheek was quite distracting, and she doubted very much he was anything dangerous at all.

But it never hurt to be too careful.

DORIS LEANED OVER AND GAVE Will a kiss, which would have been welcome if not for the fact that he was driving in four lanes of traffic at the time.

"No," he said, laughing. "Sit down."

The small collie—or whatever breed she was—sat, but her feathered tail wagged against the back of the passenger seat. She didn't seem to mind riding in the car. In fact, Will swore the little brown-and-white dog knew exactly what was going on and couldn't wait to get to the airport. He'd wanted to get his mother a purebred collie pup for Christmas, like the one his father had given her before they were married. He'd thought she would like the company, especially now that he was spending so much time in Washington, but instead he'd been convinced by a co-worker to give abandoned Doris—mature, spayed and house-broken—a home.

"You'll like the ranch," he told the dog, putting more pressure on the gas pedal. "I'm gonna get a big red bow for you, too, but first we have to get on that plane."

Doris—named by the woman who'd rescued her—whined, but leapt to the floor of the car and curled up on Will's biggest bath towel to wait out the rest of the trip to Dulles.

It was the last quiet moment that Will was going to experience for the rest of the day, because once he'd parked his car in the long-term parking lot, Doris refused to walk on her leash. The sounds of the airplanes roaring overhead scared her, so much so that she did nothing but shiver and pee while they waited for the shuttle to arrive.

The driver wasn't pleased when he saw the small collie. "She's not going to pee in my bus, is she?"

"Heck, no," Will said, hoping he was telling the truth. "She's much too well behaved for that."

Doris didn't want to get on the bus, so Will had to carry her up the steps, leave her in the aisle of the bus, then retrieve his duffel bag and the dog crate. By the time he sat on the bench, Doris sitting regally between his knees, Will was covered with strands of white-and-brown dog hair and praying that he wouldn't miss his plane.

It didn't get any easier, because the small collie didn't want to get in her crate, didn't want to walk on her brand-new red leash and barked at the security guards flanking the double doors to the main terminal's entrance. Getting to the Northwest ticket counter took more time than Will could afford, but once he'd paid the extra money to have Doris accompany him on the flight to Great Falls, Montana, he figured the worst was over.

Until Dylan Briggs caught up with him, that is. She was out of breath, which meant she must have been rushing as much as he'd been. This time she wore slim black slacks, black boots and a long ivory sweater. All that golden hair was pulled back into a ponytail. This was one very odd, very beautiful woman, and Will had the sinking feeling that Dylan wasn't here to wish him bon voyage.

Doris wagged her tail at her, and Dylan bent down to pat her head.

"Nice dog," she said. "Is she going on the plane with us?"

"Us?" He peered at her head. The earrings that dangled from her lobes looked like reindeer with rhinestones on their antlers. She had a beautiful neck, and if it was evening and he had taken her out for drinks, he would lean over and kiss some of that soft skin. And get a reindeer in his eyeball, most likely. "There's no 'us.'"

She waved a Northwest ticket envelope in front of him. "I'm going where you and the dog are going."

"I don't have time for this," he muttered, and attempted to lead Doris toward the security line. Once again the little dog refused to budge, so Will picked her up and tucked her under his arm. He slung his small duffel over his shoulder and picked up the crate. "Excuse me."

"Look," she said, hurrying after him. "I think we got off on the wrong foot this morning."

"Not a problem," he said, looking for a clock. Sure enough, time was ticking away at an alarming speed. He walked faster. The airport was crowded with holiday travelers, which made it difficult to negotiate the crowds without hitting people with Doris's crate.

"And I'd like to apologize for my, um, attitude this morning."

"Sure." He looked over to see that she was keeping

up with him. She rolled a black suitcase behind her, held a long coat folded over her arm and one of those little purses bounced beneath her right breast. "How did you know where I was?"

"Your tickets were on the coffee table. Northwest Airlines Flight 617, departs 11:05 a.m. from Dulles and arrives in Great Falls at 5:38 p.m. One connection at Salt Lake City," she recited.

"How'd you get a ticket so fast? I thought all the flights were booked solid."

"My Visa card helped. And so did a phone call to a friend of mine who works at Northwest Airlines."

"And this is important to you because?" He found the end of a line that looked longer than a football field and stood behind a gray-haired woman who wore too much perfume. Dylan stepped right in alongside of him.

"Because I have to know that Mel is all right."

"And you won't take my word for it, obviously."

"You're a total stranger. Why should I?"

"Look," Will said, setting down the crate so he could get a better grip on the dog. "Any minute now I'm going to start thinking that you're a stalker." Though he didn't think a woman who looked like Dylan needed to stalk anyone. He'd seen at least four men stare at her as they'd crossed the terminal. He, on the other hand, got dirty looks because he was carrying a dog. For some reason his fellow travelers weren't animal lovers.

Doris stretched up and licked his chin, then cried to get down. Will tightened his grip, knowing the dog would most likely pee on someone's suitcase as soon as her paws hit the floor.

"She's growling at you, poor thing." Dylan gave the dog's back a tentative pat.

"That's not a growl. It's a whine."

"Whatever. The poor baby isn't happy."

"Look around," he said, as the collie thrust her nose into his Adam's apple. "Nobody is."

She did, and Will saw two approaching businessmen try to make eye contact with her.

"True," she admitted. "There aren't a lot of happy campers here this morning. I myself could use a cup of coffee." She set her suitcase beside his leg. "Hold my place in line and I'll get us some."

He leaned over and saw that the security checkpoint was still a ways off, but the line was moving steadily. "You'd better make it fast."

"I will. What do you take in yours?"

"Black. One sugar." Though how he could drink coffee and hold Doris at the same time was a mystery.

When Dylan returned, less than five minutes later, she was followed by a young Starbucks employee who looked like he was in love. He carried a cardboard tray with six cups of coffee pressed into the indentations, which he held for Dylan to distribute.

"Here, Mr. Stone, this one is yours, I think." She smiled prettily and handed him a cup that, despite its plastic cover, smelled like freshly ground coffee beans.

"Thanks." Doris tried to sniff it, but he held it out of reach of her long nose.

Melanie turned to the people in line behind them. "Would anyone like coffee?"

"Bless you," one middle-aged woman declared. "What a lovely thing to do."

"It's Christmas," Dylan said, distributing the other three cups to the closest people in line. She gave the Starbucks kid a five-dollar tip, wished him a happy holiday and took the last cup out of the tray. "There," she said, turning to Will. "Isn't this nice?"

No, he thought. This was insane.

2

DORIS DIDN'T WANT TO GO inside her crate. Dylan watched as Will attempted to scoot the dog headfirst into the carrier, but Doris was stubborn. She cried, then howled as if he was hurting her. Several people muttered their disapproval, but there really wasn't anything else the man could do. The little dog associated the crate with an unpleasant experience and obviously preferred to travel on her own four feet.

"Will she fit in there?" Dylan wasn't convinced that this was the way for Doris to travel, either.

"The alternative is in the cargo area of the plane, which sounded too damn risky to me. Besides, she's more hair than body," he said. "The lady I got her from said this would work."

"You mean you've never done this before?"

"She's a Christmas present for my mother. A woman in my office works at an animal shelter and, well, one thing led to another. It's a long story."

Well, that put a different spin on things. The dog clearly wasn't a specific breed, at least nothing Dylan had ever seen before, and she wasn't a puppy. So the cowboy was taking a rescued dog to his mom for Christmas?

"Your mother must love dogs," she managed to say as she scooted down to hold the crate. "She's not a puppy?"

"No. The shelter thought she was around four or five."

"Come on, sweetie," Dylan crooned to Doris. "You can do it."

Doris whined, but when her attention focused on Dylan, who made kissy noises, Will was eventually able to move her into the crate.

And, as the security guard explained, "that mutt" needed to be crated from now on. That was, until they reached the checkpoint to have their bags checked, meaning Doris had to be removed from her crate and carried by Will through the machine.

All in all, it ate up valuable time. Dylan was asked to step aside for the wand check, while Doris barked her displeasure at the rancher and everyone around the security tables. It took forever to reach the concourse, and when they found the assigned gate, not one passenger remained in the waiting area.

"This doesn't look good," Will muttered.

"What's going on?" Dylan came to a stop beside Will and waited for the Delta gate agent to explain why the door was closed.

"I'm sorry," the woman said after looking at Will's ticket. "It's our new policy. You must be here to board the plane twenty minutes before your flight or we have the right to deny access."

The cowboy frowned. "Could you *un*-deny access? We had delays in the security line."

She shook her head. "I'm sorry."

Will sighed. "I can see the plane right out the window over there. I really can't get on it?"

"No. But if you'll give me your ticket again, I'll see what we can do to rebook you on another flight."

"We're together." Dylan placed her ticket on the counter next to Will's.

After all the trouble she'd gone to, they had missed the plane, but that didn't mean they couldn't get to Great Falls. And Great Falls, Dylan had decided, was exactly where she wanted to be. At least for a few days. She'd book a suite in the city's best hotel and have a grand old Christmas with Mel and Beth.

"I also have a dog with me," Will said.

"On this plane?"

"No. She rides with me. In her crate. At my feet."

The ticket agent didn't look pleased. "And you're sure she will fit under the seat? Regulations require—"

"Absolutely," Dylan broke in. "She travels all the time and she's very well behaved. Our Doris is from a long line of champions."

"Oh?" The woman peered over the desk to see. "What kind of dog is that?"

"Well," Will drawled. "She's not exactly—"

"A Miniature Tourister Montana Collie," Dylan announced with great conviction. She didn't know exactly why, but teasing the cowboy was a good enough reason. And she didn't want anyone telling them that Doris couldn't travel, too.

"Wow," the woman said. "I've never seen one of those before."

Will turned to frown, but Dylan ignored him. "When's the next flight to Great Falls?"

After typing furiously, frowning and typing again, the Delta agent announced she could get them on a flight "at six-twenty-five, arriving in Great Falls at 11:25, with a stopover in Salt Lake."

"There's nothing sooner?" This was from Will, who looked less than thrilled about waiting another six hours.

"There's an American flight to Chicago at 2:34," she said, studying the screen. "Leaving Chicago at 4:39, arrives Minneapolis at 6:09. Connects with a Northwest flight out of Minneapolis, arriving in Great Falls at ten. You can try them to see if they have any space, but it's going to cost you."

"Thanks. I'll try that," he said.

"There aren't many seats open on our six-thirty flight, so come back right away if you can't get on another flight."

"Thank you," Dylan said, retrieving her ticket. She turned to Will, who had picked up the dog crate and his duffel bag and was already halfway into the main corridor.

"Hey," she called, hurrying after him. "Where are you going?"

"To an American counter." He carried the crate and the bag as if they weighed nothing at all. And he was a particularly handsome man, even wearing scuffed cowboy boots and blue jeans. But he wasn't all cowboy, not with a white oxford shirt and a tweedy sports coat and a worn leather belt. He looked like a man completely at ease with himself. He acted like a man who wanted to go home. To her cousin?

She followed Will as best she could through the crowds, stood beside him at the American Airlines counter and, after he'd purchased a ticket, whipped out her Visa card and paid for one of the last remaining seats on Flight 1263.

"There," the cowboy said, moving away from the counter and parking Doris's crate on a seat in the waiting area. "I'm glad that's done. Me and my Miniature Tourister Montana Collie can go home today, after all." He gave her a rare smile. "Where the hell did you come up with that name?"

Dylan pointed to her suitcase, clearly labeled American Tourister. "I didn't want the woman to give Doris a hard time. The poor thing is having a hard day."

"Tell me about it," he muttered, bending down to see the dog. "You'd better be worth the trouble, girl."

"Are you talking to me or Doris?" Dylan quipped, and the cowboy straightened.

"Well, that's a good question, I guess. I know why this dog is going to my ranch. But I don't know what you're doing."

"I told you. I want to make sure Melanie is all right."

"You could do that with a phone call."

"I think she's turned her cell off."

"Give me your ticket." He reached into his inside jacket pocket and pulled out a pen. When she gave him the envelope, he scrawled something on the back and handed it back to her. "That's the phone number at the ranch. Call Melanie and stop worrying. Just remember there's a two-hour time difference, so it's only nine-fifteen there now."

"Thank you."

"You're welcome. It's been...interesting meeting you," he said, sitting down beside the dog crate as if he was not going to move until it was time to get on the plane. "And I hope you have a nice Christmas."

"I'm sure I will," Dylan said. *I'll be in Great Falls with the only members of my family who aren't partying on a cruise ship instead of singing around the Christmas tree.*

He looked relieved, which was a little insulting.

Dylan wasn't used to that sort of expression from men.

"Bye, Doris," she said to the dog, whose nose was pressed against the gray plastic crate. She turned back to the cowboy. "Do you want me to bring you anything? I don't know about you, but I didn't have time for breakfast this morning."

"You mean you're coming *back*?"

"Of course. After I eat." She tucked her ticket into her tote bag. "I've always wanted to see Big Sky country. That's what people call Montana, isn't it?"

"In tourist brochures."

"See you in a little while." She'd forgotten her coffee at the security table and, thanks to the flight from Paris and a six-hour time difference, had been awake for approximately thirty hours. Being overtired made her silly.

Needing caffeine made her dangerous.

And missing her family made her desperate to get on any plane at all.

HIS FRIENDS WOULD CALL HIM crazy to want to get rid of Dylan Briggs. His brother would laugh at him. And Uncle Joe would say something like, "If I was thirty years younger..."

But all that aside, Dylan Briggs was a beautiful woman. Not the kind of woman he would normally avoid, of course. He liked her looks, though her sense of humor was a bit bizarre. Still, she hadn't thrown hissy fits over waiting in line, missing a plane or dealing with Doris. Aside from her protective attitude toward Melanie, Dylan Briggs appeared to be an interesting woman.

But not today. Today he didn't have the time or the energy for flirting, seduction or anything else that involved any kind of effort. He just wanted to take Doris and go home. He wanted to see how his brother, Jared, and their houseguest were getting along. He wanted to tease his mother about having a baby in the house again, play gin rummy with Joe and help Aunt Bitty change the batteries on her Walkman. He'd been gone since Thanksgiving, and though he enjoyed his work in D.C., he missed the ranch.

He missed home.

And he was hungry. Doris whined, so Will let her out of her crate and hooked her up to a leash. An airline worker told him where to walk her, down a set of metal stairs to a baggage-car area, and Doris hurried to pee exactly where he suggested she do it. Then she pranced in circles until Will took a dog biscuit from his pocket and gave it to her.

"You're easier to get along with than some people I know," he told her. The little dog, twenty pounds of hair and good humor, wagged her tail again.

So far so good, only he was getting hungry. He should have taken Dylan up on her offer of food, but he didn't want to encourage her to think they were traveling companions. Hell, he hoped she'd have called Melanie by now and realized that her worries were unfounded, that her cousin had decided to spend Christmas where she could forget her grief and not see pity reflected on the faces of those who loved her. He'd been trying to do the woman a favor, considering she was the only one of his neighbors who'd gone out of her way to be nice to a stranger, but he never suspected that Melanie's cousin would come trailing along, too.

He'd thought his sweet little neighbor should meet Jared, and if ever there was a man who needed to meet a woman like Melanie, it was his older brother.

Too bad he couldn't figure out how to do the same thing for himself.

DORIS SAT PROUDLY ON the cowboy's lap while the man talked into his cell phone. Probably explaining his delayed arrival to some little woman who baked bread and cooked up those home-grown steaks, Dylan figured.

Carrying a paper bag and rolling her suitcase behind her, she walked over to a row of empty seats across the wide aisle from where Will sat and settled in for the next couple of hours. She had food, coffee, the latest issue of *Victoria* magazine and a *New York Times* bestselling paperback novel about a serial killer. Nearby, a wall-hung television recited the latest news, while outside the sky was overcast, though that didn't seem to stop planes from arriving.

She had a pretty good view of the cowboy. He seemed oblivious to the curious looks heading his way. A little boy escaped his mother's hold and ran over to say hello to the dog. Doris took it all in stride, but Dylan noticed that the cowboy's large hand tightened on the dog's chest, as if telling her to be careful. He put his phone back in his pocket and talked to the little boy. Two little girls, about eight or nine, became brave enough to venture over to pet the dog, too, while Will talked to all of them and ignored the fact that the dog's feathered tail wagged against his crotch.

Well, cowboys were used to dealing with animals. But as this particular cowboy chuckled at something the little boy said, Dylan felt an unfamiliar tug at her heart.

Which she set out to ignore.

WILL TOLD HIMSELF THAT it wasn't up to him to do anything, that it would be much easier to walk away and let the woman miss the flight to Chicago. But in the end he couldn't do it.

Not because he was a nice guy, but because he couldn't get Doris into the crate without Dylan's help.

So he picked up his bag, his crate and his dog and crossed over to the opposite gate. Dylan lay across three seats, her eyes closed, her head on her tote bag and her little purse tucked under her side. The suit-case sat in front of her and one hand draped over the extended handle, as if she thought that those delicate fingers—ringless, he noted with passing interest—would be enough to deter a thief.

"Hey," he said. "Wake up."

Miss I-Just-Got-in-from-Paris didn't budge. Out cold, he surmised, from her resemblance to a corpse. He ran his index finger along the back of her hand. Nothing.

He leaned closer, tapped her shoulder, spoke into her ear, but the woman didn't move. Some of that streaky yellow hair lay across her cheek, so he gave in to temptation and swept it aside so he could see her closed eyelids. She was much more attractive when she wasn't giving him a difficult time.

"We're now boarding passengers in rows twelve and higher for American Flight 1263, to Chicago. Please have your boarding passes ready for the gate attendant."

Will looked across the concourse to see that the line of people boarding the plane was moving right along, so he gave Dylan's arm another shake and called her name. "Hey, Dylan! Wake up!"

Doris, tucked under his arm and deciding that this was a fun game, began to bark and wag her tail as if she couldn't wait to get down and play.

"No," he told her. "Bad dog."

"Don't say that," Dylan said drowsily. "You'll hurt her feelings."

"You want to get on the plane or not?"

Her eyes flew open and she sat up. "What?"

"We're leaving," Will explained. "It's after two o'clock. How long have you been asleep?"

She reached up and took the dog from him. "Not long enough. Hey, girl, do you want to go for a ride?"

Doris's tail wiggled its approval of the word *ride*.

"She won't get in the crate and we're running out of time."

Dylan glanced toward the gate. "We have plenty of time," she said. "Our little Miniature Tourister Montana Collie can't miss Christmas on the ranch." She rummaged through her tote bag and pulled out a piece of chocolate chip cookie.

"I already tried that with a dog biscuit."

She ignored him. "When I was a kid I had a dog who loved these." She held it up for Doris to sniff, but she didn't give it to her. "Put the crate down on the floor."

He did as he was told and opened the end door. Then Dylan handed him a small piece of cookie. "Toss that inside and see if she'll go in after it."

Which, of course, worked. Meaning, if he'd thought of bribery himself, he could have left the blonde sleeping in Dulles.

3

THE FACT THAT THE TWO females in Will's company slept all the way to Chicago was, in Will's opinion, an unexpected bonus in an otherwise stressful day. Doris curled up in her crate, closed her eyes and settled into a deep sleep. There were even moments when Will thought he heard snoring coming from the vicinity of his boots.

Dylan had appropriated three pillows and a blanket from the overhead compartment before they stored their bags and coats, settled herself in the window seat, refused the flight attendant's offer of a drink and pretzels and closed her eyes. There was no snoring.

In that respect, she was the perfect traveling companion.

On the other hand, he wouldn't have minded knowing more about her. Like what she was doing in Paris and if there was a man in her life.

Her personal life was none of his business—or maybe it was, considering she appeared to be heading to the ranch—but he couldn't help being curious. If she lived with someone she hadn't mentioned him.

And she didn't want to spend Christmas with a boy-friend...or his family, which meant she most likely wasn't engaged, with or without a ring. Melanie had said her cousin was some kind of interior decorator, with an office in Georgetown and a devoted clientele who paid a lot of money for old furniture.

He could believe it. This particular female looked glamorous, expensive and high-maintenance, like most of the women he'd met in D.C. He didn't exactly live like a monk and he did enjoy the social life the city had to offer, but his stays in D.C. had become much of the same thing over and over again: expensive dinners with ambitious people. The women were beautiful, intelligent and ambitious. Not that there was anything wrong with ambition, but lately he'd longed to stay home and watch a football game with a woman who was happy with take-out pizza and a bag of Oreo cookies.

He guessed that was why he liked Melanie so much. She'd even let him hold the baby, and once, when she'd had to go to the store, she'd agreed to let him stay with the sleeping baby. He was the trust-worthy type, all right. And Melanie was like a younger sister—a younger sister who'd had more than her share of tragedy.

Unlike her cousin. He glanced over at the sleeping dynamo. Nope. Not his type at all, he decided, tear-ing open his bag of pretzels.

Dylan shifted as if she was trying to get comfortable. She ended up leaning close to him, her knee against his thigh and her face inches from his shoulder. An unused pillow tumbled to the floor. Will waved to the flight attendant for another bag of pretzels. He should have eaten more than a bagel and an apple at Dulles, because he was getting strangely light-headed.

"DAMN IT ALL TO HELL."

Dylan didn't have to open her eyes to know that the cowboy was upset. She'd been awake since the plane began to descend, when the pilot announced their arrival at O'Hare and thanked them for flying with American. But she'd kept her eyes closed and her forehead on Will Stone's arm, where she'd landed sometime during the flight. He smelled like soap and some kind of aftershave with a hint of musk. She wondered if he smelled like that all over his body or just his shirt—before she reminded herself to act her age.

"Hey," he said, a little softer. His breath tickled her forehead. He muttered something about "like trying to wake the dead" and gave her arm a gentle shake. "We've landed."

"That was fast," she murmured, sitting up and blinking to clear her vision. "How's Doris?"

"Asleep."

"Good doggy," she said to the crate, then looked at

Will. "How do you take her to the bathroom before we get on the next plane?"

"I'll get someone to let me go outside."

She turned to the window and lifted the shade. "It's snowing."

"Yeah," he said. "I know. You missed the announcement that some flights have been canceled."

"Ours?"

"Probably. It's not like we're flying to Miami."

So that explained the swearing. Still, the snow didn't look too heavy. It wasn't as if the runways were covered with snow and even if they were, Dylan could see snowplows lined up at the end of the concourse. "They didn't say anything specific about Minneapolis?"

"No. We're to check the monitors when we get out onto the concourse."

Dylan waited for the plane to come to a stop before she pulled out her cell phone from the bag at her feet. Her assistant answered on the first ring, took her instructions and promised to call back with details.

"Thanks," she said, pushing the end button.

"You booked a hotel room here?" The cowboy looked surprised, as if he'd never heard of "thinking ahead." "Isn't that a little pessimistic?"

"The next time I go to sleep I'd like to be in a bed," she explained, rubbing a sore spot on her neck. "With clean sheets and big fat pillows and a nice comfy mattress." She sighed, half hoping the traveling day was over. "And if Chicago is snowed in, I want to make sure I get one of the hotel rooms before they're all booked up. I can cancel it later on if I don't need it."

"Melanie said you were smart."

"Sometimes, sometimes not," she said, over the sound of seat belts clicking open. But she was smart enough not to be tempted by a handsome face, a muscled body and a well-worn pair of cowboy boots. Smart enough to ignore the smile of a good-looking rancher who had gentle hands and an easy way with dogs.

And certainly smart enough to keep up with the man from Montana after he retrieved their possessions from the overhead bin, picked up his dog and loped off the plane.

But once they stood in front of the bank of monitors, it was clear that the news wasn't good. Their flight to Minneapolis was delayed an hour and a half, which meant they were stuck once again. They took turns visiting the rest rooms and even managed to find an outside entrance for Doris to relieve herself, which ate up about twenty minutes. The concrete was slippery—even Will lost his balance and almost fell— and Doris made it clear she didn't care for ice under her feet, but Dylan was grateful for a few minutes of fresh air.

"Come on," Dylan said, once they were back inside. "I'll buy you a drink." He looked as if he was going to refuse, but instead he picked up Doris and his bag and followed her into the crowded lounge. A television blared from above the bar, but it was only ESPN news and nothing about the weather.

Dylan saw three businessmen leaving a table on the outside edge of the bar and claimed it. Doris sat at Will's feet and looked glad to be out of the crate. Will shoved the bags between his chair and Dylan's, then leaned back to look around the lounge. "This was a good idea," he said.

"I've never been in a bar with a cowboy before."

"Rancher," Will corrected, then smiled to show that he knew she was only teasing. "You don't know what you're missing. I could start line-dancing any minute."

The waitress came over to take their order and looked at Doris, who wagged her tail. "You can't have a dog in here."

"That's not just any dog," Will said, giving her a smile that would melt ice. "She's a champion Miniature Tourister Montana Collie."

"Yeah?" The girl, who in Dylan's eyes didn't look old enough to serve drinks, returned the cowboy's smile. "So what does that make you?"

"Thirsty," he said. "You don't mind, do you?"

"I guess not." She leaned closer. "What'll you have?"

Will looked at Dylan, who replied, "A vodka tonic, please. A double." She'd never ordered a "double" of anything, not since college, anyway. With any luck, she'd sleep on the next flight, too. Maybe she'd use the cowboy as a pillow again.

"Bring me a beer," Will said. "Whatever you have on tap is fine."

"Sure." Another flirty look. "Just keep the dog from bothering anybody, okay?"

Dylan waited for the waitress to leave before speaking. "Line-dancing?"

He shrugged, but his brown eyes twinkled. "I do a mean two-step, too. Do you dance?"

"Not really. I had a bad experience at ballet class when I was five."

He laughed. Which was a very pleasant sound. "I could teach you."

Oh, yes, she thought. *I'll just bet you could.* Dylan had a vision of learning all sorts of things from this man, but quickly banished them. What was the matter with her? She attempted to change the subject. "So, on your ranch do you ride horses and brand cattle and fix fences?"

"Sure," Will began, but was distracted when the waitress returned and Dylan paid for the drinks before he could find his wallet.

"My treat," was all she said, lifting her drink. "Here's hoping we're in Montana tonight."

He clicked his beer mug against her glass. "I'll drink to that, sweetheart."

She didn't know why the endearment pleased her, but Dylan hoped the vodka would knock some sense into her.

WILL STOOD NEXT TO DYLAN and watched as she gave her name to the clerk at the hotel's reservations desk. A long line of people stretched behind them, as the airport was now officially closed due to bad weather. As she waited for the man to finish the paperwork, she tapped her credit card on the counter and turned to Will.

"Do you get the feeling this isn't your best day?"

"Yes, ma'am," Will said, using his best western drawl. The truth was this had become the Day from Hell, no exaggeration, because when he'd gone to pay for a second round of drinks in the lounge, things had gone from bad to worse—Will had done the unexplainable and lost his wallet. Meaning his Visa, driver's license, two hundred in cash and various other papers were gone. He thought the wallet might have slipped from the pocket of his jacket one of the thirty or forty times he'd bent over Doris. Maybe outside, back in Dulles. The airline was looking for it; security in both airports were aware that someone might have a fake ID.

They had stood in too many lines for too long, but they'd been re-ticketed for a flight to Great Falls—via Salt Lake—in the morning. Will looked at Dylan and tried to make the best of things. "I call missing a plane, getting stuck in Chicago and losing my wallet three ingredients for a pretty bad day. But it's not going to spoil my Christmas."

"Thanks for not adding me onto your list."

"I would have," he said, "but my mother taught me to be polite."

"Please let me get you a room," Dylan said. "You can pay me back when you get to the ranch." She turned to the hotel clerk, who looked frazzled and tired. "Can I have another room for the night?"

"No, ma'am." His gaze darted to Will, who hoped like hell that the kid hadn't seen Doris in her crate and wasn't going to use the "no pets" rule to refuse him a bed. He also hoped that Doris wouldn't start whining and call attention to herself. "We're booked solid now that the airport has shut down. I'm sending people to other hotels around the area. If you go to the main terminal and check with the information desk—"

"Thank you anyway," Dylan said, moving out of the line. She held her key card in her hand. "I guess you'd better sleep with me." Then she blushed. "I didn't mean it like that."

"No, that's okay. I'll figure something out."

"But Doris—"

"Will be fine." And good company, too, as long as she didn't pee on his boots.

"She can stay with me, you know. You both can." Dylan looked nervous over the idea and he couldn't blame her. But he did give her credit for offering to give a stranger a place to sleep.

"Thanks," he said. "But no."

"I'll buy you two some dinner."

"I still have some cash." About twenty dollars, which wasn't going to go far but would get him a meal. He ran his fingers through his hair and hoped like hell that whoever had his wallet hadn't been busy charging big-screen televisions and trips to Vegas on his Visa card before it was canceled. "Don't worry. I'll see you in the morning. Around eight?"

"Come on, cowboy." Dylan attempted to lift the dog crate, but didn't get it very far off the ground. She hung on, though, and tilted to one side and moved toward the bank of elevators. "Let's find my room. We'll order a couple of steaks and watch the rodeo competition on ESPN. Isn't that what you guys from Montana do for fun?"

He caught up with her in two strides and took the dog crate from her. "Not when we're with our women, we don't."

"It's no use trying to sweet-talk me," she said. "Not until I've ordered room service and broken into the minibar."

"I think you've had a little too much to drink already." Come to think of it, Dylan Briggs wasn't quite herself. For one thing, she wobbled. And when the elevator lifted, she closed her eyes and fell backward into the corner. He figured the jet lag must have caught up with her, because she looked like the kind of woman who could hold her liquor better than this.

"Whoa, there, sweetheart." He took her elbow and helped her get balanced, much to the amusement of an elderly couple sharing the elevator with them.

The old man gave him a sympathetic nod. "Some weather, eh?"

"Sure is." The elevator doors opened at the tenth floor and the couple moved to leave.

"Hope your wife's feeling better," the lady said. "She looks awfully tired."

Dylan's eyes flew open. "I'm not—"

"She's had a real long day," Will interrupted. "She just needs a good night's sleep." He wondered just how much vodka she'd drunk. Since they'd left the lounge to discover their flight had been canceled, Dylan had seemed pretty cheerful. She'd discussed the merits of off-season travel with a middle-aged couple heading to London in January, debated the validity of the BCS poll with a hefty kid who wore a Tennessee Volunteers football jersey, and even chatted about pets with a young woman traveling with her cat. Pudgie, he thought the cat's name was.

"I *have* had a real long day," Dylan said, echoing his words as the elevator door shut and they were alone. "Have you ever been to France?"

"No."

"Too bad. I love the wine. And the cognac. Do they drink cognac in Montana?"

Wonderful. Now he was traveling with an alcoholic.

"Maybe you'd better lighten up on the booze," he said, grabbing her arm again.

"I'm just nervous. Or maybe it's jet lag," she said, but she closed her eyes again. "I've been getting dizzy since this morning."

"Keep your eyes open, sweetheart. This is your floor." The doors parted and Will grabbed everything but Dylan's rolling suitcase, which she managed easily by herself.

"I'm sorry," she whispered. "I never could hold my liquor. That's a bad thing in the West, isn't it."

"A man could hang for less. What's your room number?"

"Wait a minute." She fumbled through her purse and pulled out the hotel info. "Fourteen-thirty-two."

He took the lead and headed down the corridor until they reached the right door at the very end. Dylan gave him the key card, he opened the door and managed to get the dog, the woman and the suitcases into the foyer. The foyer? Will looked around the corner to see a huge green-and-cream-colored living room. Two sofas, two armchairs and a low glass table took up most of the space. Beyond that was a large window, its drapes pulled shut against the storm. A desk and armoire lined one of the long walls; there was a telephone and an assortment of hotel information on the desk.

Dylan disappeared through a nearby door and returned smiling. "Remind me to give my assistant another Christmas bonus."

"Because?" He squatted down to open the door to Doris's crate. The little dog tumbled out as fast as her little legs could move, then shook herself.

"She booked me a suite. A heavenly suite. There's a nice big bedroom in there." She waved one arm toward the living room area. "And I'll bet one of those sofas opens up to a bed, so you don't have to act like a martyr and sleep in the airport."

"I was behaving like a gentleman, not a martyr," he pointed out. "Hey, don't pee on the carpet," he said as the dog trotted over to the couch and sniffed one of the mahogany legs.

"Do you think she understands what you said?" Dylan sat down on the nearest couch, pulled off her boots and set her stocking feet on the coffee table.

"I sure as hell hope so." His stomach growled. "Did you mean what you said about ordering room service or was that the alcohol talking?"

"Order whatever you want, as long as I don't have to get up off this couch. Okay, Doris, come on." She patted the couch cushion and Doris hopped up to join her. "This dog has great manners. Why would she have been dumped in an animal shelter?"

"Her former owner wanted to travel."

"That's a lousy excuse to get rid of a pet."

"Yeah, but she'll like the ranch once I get her there.

What do you want to eat?" He picked up the room service menu and the telephone, which had a long cord, and sat down on the couch opposite her. "Room service consists of sirloin burgers, steak sandwiches, chicken fingers, salads and cold sandwiches, like roast beef, tuna fish, egg salad and peanut butter and jelly."

"What about desserts?"

"'Ask us for details on our tempting assortment of pies and cakes or choose from the list of toppings for a triple-scoop sundae,'" he read. "The toppings are hot fudge, chocolate sauce, caramel and strawberry sauce."

"I want a hamburger with mushrooms and French fries," she said. "I'll share it with Doris. And chocolate cake, if they have it. Or cheesecake with strawberries."

"You got it." He thought he might have the same thing. And maybe a piece of pie.

"I am so happy to be out of airports and planes," she murmured. Doris had tipped over on her back and spread her legs for a tummy rub, which Dylan provided.

Will picked up the telephone receiver. He'd better keep his mind on food or he'd be over on the couch looking for some physical attention himself.

4

AFTER DINNER DYLAN TURNED into a domestic whirlwind. Not only did she discover that the drapes hid glass doors to an enclosed balcony—perfect for Doris's convenience, she pointed out—but in the bedroom closet were sheets, pillows and two blankets for the sofa that did indeed open out into a queen-size bed.

"Voilà," she announced, tossing the couch cushions onto the floor. She pointed to the mattress frame underneath. "Your bed, cowboy."

"Yes, ma'am," was all Will replied. He wasn't going to argue any longer. They rearranged the furniture and turned the living room into his bedroom. Any images of Dylan's bed with Dylan in it were immediately squashed. After all, the two of them weren't exactly a match made in heaven.

They weren't even a match at all.

"I wonder how my brother is doing entertaining your cousin," he said, unfolding a sheet. "Jared must have been real surprised when he saw her."

She stopped unfolding a blanket to look at him. "Is that what all this was about? You're *matchmaking?*"

"Well—" He didn't realize it would be so apparent. "Melanie and my brother don't know what I'm up to. He thinks I invited a friend to the ranch for Christmas, that's all. I told him to take good care of her. She's...his type."

"And all day I've thought you were after her yourself." She flapped the blanket and tossed it over his bed.

"I thought about it," he admitted, remembering the first time he'd met Melanie. She'd been trying to get the baby carriage into the elevator of their building. In a very unmaternal gesture, she'd kicked the elevator door with her foot and swore. "For about two minutes."

"And then what?"

"She didn't attract me like that."

"Meaning?" Those blue eyes were very curious and Will tried not to squirm.

"Well," he sighed. "We became friends. I couldn't picture anything more, uh, intimate." There. Maybe now she'd stop asking questions.

"I guess you met her when you moved into that building." Dylan stopped making the bed and waited for more details. She had that protective look on her face again, as if she thought he was up to no good. "She's lived there for years...with her fiancé."

"I helped her with the elevator one afternoon."

"And you know about—what happened, why she

and Beth are alone?'' She crossed her arms in front of her and rubbed, as if she was cold.

"Yes." Melanie had eventually told him about the plane crash. She'd also told him a lot of other things, including the fact that she wanted to get away to a place where no one knew what happened. "She wanted to go away for a while, she said, which was one of the reasons I invited her out to the ranch."

"And the other reason was your brother. What's he like?" Dylan bent over and tucked another corner of the blanket under the foam.

"Jared? Quiet. Steady. The kind of man anyone would want for a brother." The last time he'd checked his cell phone there'd been two messages from his older brother demanding a return phone call. Well, Jared could wait. Will had done what he could by putting his brother and Melanie together; the rest was up to them. He figured Jared wouldn't be able to resist her—and if Jared wasn't going to get off the ranch and find himself a woman, then Will would have to send him one.

"What's so funny?"

He looked up from a haphazard bed-making job. "Was I smiling?"

"Yes."

"I was trying to picture how Jared was reacting to Melanie. My brother tends to be shy around women."

"I guess that's not a family trait."

Will chuckled. "Not exactly. You should meet my uncle Joe. He's still a lady-killer at eighty-two."

"Does he live on the ranch, too?"

"No, but he likes to visit. He's the only family my mother has left, so she likes having him around."

"And what about Mel?" Dylan hugged the bed pillow to her chest as if she were trying to comfort herself. He couldn't believe she was worried about Melanie's reception at Graystone. She and the baby would be treated like royalty.

"My mother couldn't be happier. She really goes all out for Christmas—cookies, decorations, presents, the whole thing." Now the woman looked as if she wanted to cry. Damn. He couldn't figure out what to say.

"Have you talked to Mel?" she asked, after a long minute of silence.

"Yes, I've called home. Several times. But I haven't talked to Melanie yet. She went to town to do some Christmas shopping this afternoon and tonight she was busy with the baby."

"So she's okay." He almost thought he heard a wistful note in her voice, but he reminded himself that this was a woman who made her own rules—which didn't include spending the holidays with her own parents. Odd, but then he figured it was none of his business.

"Yeah," he assured her. "They all are."

His mother had sounded pretty pleased with the

company, though disappointed she wasn't going to have the entire family together tonight. But she wasn't the kind to make mountains out of molehills. She had been a rancher's wife and they were a tough breed.

Sort of like the woman making his bed.

IT WAS ALL DORIS'S FAULT. She couldn't decide which person to sleep with, so even though she started off the night curled up at the cowboy's feet, she ended up whining at Dylan's closed bedroom door.

For some reason Dylan couldn't sleep, either. She'd watched the news (too depressing), the Weather Channel (too cold), old episodes of *X-Files* (too scary) and finally, a cowboy movie. While she watched John Wayne—at least that's who she thought the star might be—lead a cattle drive to some town with a railroad, Dylan tried not to think of the cowboy who was sleeping on the other side of the wall.

And when Doris's whines escalated to the point where Dylan heard them over the sound of mooing cows and John Wayne's gunshots, she slid out of bed and headed to the door to see what was the matter.

"Doris?"

The little dog wagged her tail twice and trotted past Dylan toward the bed. Then, without so much as a "please, may I" hopped up on the bed and wriggled under the covers.

"Well, make yourself comfortable," she muttered,

but she was actually glad for the company. "Do you like westerns?"

"Why?" came the male voice behind her. "What's on?"

She turned back to the door to see Will standing there clad in a white T-shirt that unfortunately covered that wide chest. Her gaze dipped lower, just to make sure he wasn't one of those men who slept naked from the waist down, but he wore dark blue sweatpants. His feet were bare, and when she looked back up to his face, she noticed his hair was rumpled.

"Oh," she said, sounding like an idiot. "It's you."

"No," he said, looking past her to the television. "It's John Wayne."

"I couldn't sleep," she admitted.

"I wouldn't have figured you for a fan of old westerns." His grin was slow, sleepy and very sexy. Dylan took a step backward. "Where is she?"

"Who?"

"The dog. I thought I heard her crying to go out."

"No." She walked over to the bed, feeling a little shy. What *was* the matter with her? "She was cold."

"Cold?"

Dylan leaned over the bed and flipped back the covers. Doris looked at them but didn't move. Her tailed wagged once, twice and then her eyes closed and she stretched out on her side as if the two of them didn't exist. "See what I mean?"

"I'll take her out of here," Will said. "I'll bet you're

not used to sleeping with Miniature Tourister Montana Collies."

"No. It's a first." And she'd never had a cowboy in her bedroom before, either. She wondered if he could read her mind, because his expression grew serious and his gaze centered on her mouth. He looked as if he wanted to say something. "What?"

"Hmm? Nothing." He sighed. Then he reached over and with his index finger touched the satin strap of her long nightgown. "I guessed you were the blue satin nightgown type, but aren't you cold?"

"No." But she shivered, anyway, which was a ridiculous reaction to a simple touch. His eyebrows rose.

"What color is this?"

"Cobalt." She reminded herself that the gown was constructed of heavy satin and therefore no more revealing than a ball gown, but the fact remained that she was naked underneath and she wasn't the only one in the room who knew it.

"Ah." His finger ever so gently touched her neck and higher, to tuck an errant strand of hair behind her ear.

"You can leave Doris with me," she managed to say, despite the lump in her throat and the fact that her heart rate had quickened at an alarming speed. "I don't mind at all."

"You don't seem like the kind of woman who sleeps with animals."

"No," she said. "I sleep alone." Let him make what he would from that. Maybe he'd stop his flirting and go back to bed.

His eyebrows rose. "Always?"

"Just about." She was not going to explain that she'd given up on all that for a while. A long while. She was not going to explain that she'd had her heart broken for the last time and from now on she intended to make her own rules and do things her own way, and any future relationships would be on her terms—which meant safe, casual and platonic.

"I'd better say good-night then," the cowboy murmured, only instead of leaving he lowered his head and kissed her. Dylan, in her satin cobalt nightgown and tingling skin, kept very still when his lips brushed hers. She would have liked to wrap her bare arms around his neck and press against that hard chest and kiss him back.

But she resisted, even though her knees felt a little wobbly.

"You're trying very hard not to kiss me back," he said, touching his lips to the corner of her mouth. "Why?"

"Because," she said, taking a step backward before she did something foolish—like tug him into her bed. "I'd rather sleep with your dog."

HE SHOULD HAVE REALIZED the problem before now, before it was too late to do anything about it. His tempting traveling companion had been quite a distraction for almost twenty-four hours, but in the cold light of dawn Will realized he had to come up with another way to get home.

Thinking about Dylan, who was now on the other side of the wall taking a shower, was not going to get him home for Christmas. He had to keep his mind off sex. Or at least try. He'd been up since dawn trying not to think about Dylan sleeping alone in that wide king-size bed. He hadn't met a woman he wanted to sleep with in months. Four months, one week and three days, to be precise. He'd started looking at couples in the parks and at the movies and in restaurants. He'd started wondering if he'd ever find the one woman who made him long to buy a wedding ring and ride off into the sunset.

He didn't think very many women would want to mix Washington with ranch life. And the women he'd met lately either saw him as a baby-making sperm-and-income provider or as an interesting sexual conquest. He didn't mind the sexual conquest part so much—what man would?—but he'd like to spend time with a woman who didn't unzip his pants on date number two. The last date he'd had, a lobbyist for the beef industry, had removed his boxer shorts with her teeth.

That had been a little intimidating, even for a rancher.

And here he was sharing a hotel room with an

overwhelmingly beautiful and bossy stranger. Yesterday had been one of those days that made a man long for some long, uncomplicated days of riding fence and checking cattle and enjoying the wide-open spaces without any hassles.

But now, with his wallet missing, he was stranded in Chicago, a long way from home, without any barbed wire or quarter horses in sight. The pot of coffee he'd ordered from room service arrived, and by the time Dylan was dressed and out of the bathroom, Will had folded up the bed, packed up his things and convinced Doris to go outside to pee in the snow that was piled up on the balcony.

"What's wrong?"

He looked up from drying Doris's paws to see Dylan drying her hair. She wore the same slim black slacks she'd worn yesterday, but this morning a silky white sweater covered the upper half of her appealing little body. He noticed her makeup was in place, her shoes were on, and the only part of her not ready for travel were the damp strands of hair that waved to her shoulders. She was quite the elegant lady, and the only thing he could think of was rumpling her up a bit.

He resisted, of course, having other things to deal with.

"I have no identification," Will announced, releasing the wriggling dog so she could trot over and greet her bedmate.

"I know." She bent over and tickled Doris's ears. "Good morning, sweetheart. You were such a good girl last night."

"She didn't keep you awake?"

"She snored," Dylan said with a smile. "But it was a quiet snore. It didn't bother me."

"How was the movie?"

"John Wayne killed all the bad guys and then Doris and I went to sleep." She looked past him to the desk against the wall. "Please tell me that's coffee."

"Yes, ma'am." He watched when she came closer and poured herself a cup.

"Thank you." She sat down on the couch and took a sip before she spoke again. "So, why the grim face?"

"No wallet means no identification, which means I can't get on a plane. Even if we were lucky enough to get seats on that first flight to Salt Lake, I wouldn't be let on the plane."

"Not even if they knew the circumstances?"

He shook his head. "I just talked to the airline."

"So what do we do now?"

"We?"

"Well, I've got the Visa card and you know the way to Montana, so what do we do next? Take the train?"

"No." He considered his options while he poured himself another cup of coffee. He would call Jared and ask him to wire money, which would only take a few hours at the most. Maybe he could even get the county sheriff to fax something that would prove his identification enough to get on a flight.

Or he could spend a few more days with Dylan.

"Let me tell you what I have in mind," he said.

IF ANYTHING WOULD KILL passion, Dylan hoped it would be a road trip. The cowboy was getting to her, in the most physical way. Nothing more, of course. But she'd given up sex over a year ago, having decided that it wasn't worth the trouble. She'd woken one morning to realize that the man asleep in her bed was not the man she wanted to spend the rest of her life with, so what was she doing with him every weekend for the past five months? She'd decided then and there to get out of the dating game and take up celibacy.

Now she wondered if that had been a wise decision, because the sight of a man in her bedroom had sent all sorts of exciting signals to parts of her body she would rather ignore.

She still flushed when she thought about that kiss. That tiny little kiss was completely unremarkable, but for some reason she couldn't stop thinking about the cowboy's mouth.

If she stopped to think about it, *really* think about it, the idea of setting off to Montana by car was insane. But then again, the sanest person she knew, her cousin Melanie, had loaded up her infant and her suitcases and her Christmas presents and set off to

Montana, too. Surely Dylan's plan to spend Christmas with Mel and Beth wasn't too odd.

Since a vehicle couldn't be rented without a credit card and a driver's license, Will made the arrangements to rent a four-wheel drive SUV. It was Dylan's credit card and Dylan's driver's license that were used to make the transaction legal.

"You're being a good sport about this," he said, leading the way out of the airport and toward the shuttle bus that would take them to the rental-car lot. He'd just picked up cash wired from the ranch, so they were now officially on their way.

"I've had enough of planes and airports for a while." She thought longingly of her small apartment and the antique gold bed she'd covered with *boutis*, the quilted whole-cloth coverlets from Provence. She wondered what Will would think if she invited him to visit her. By the time this adventure was over, she doubted if they would ever want to see each other again. The thought made her sad.

"Why were you in Paris?" he said, interrupting her musing.

His interest pleased her. "It was a buying trip. I go at least four times a year to see the new fabrics and find old ones. I keep a list of things that my clients are looking for, so it's similar to a treasure hunt." The cold hit them when they walked onto the sidewalk waiting area, and Doris, tucked in her crate, barked her request to leave the crate and explore the outdoors.

Will set the bags down and did just that, attaching the leash to the dog's collar and letting her sniff a cement column. She squatted on a patch of snow, trotted in happy circles around the suitcases, wagged her tail at other people who stopped to see if they were in the right place.

Dylan looked at the overcast sky, at the freshly plowed road, at the piles of snow pushed against wire fencing. "What if we run into another snowstorm?"

"We'll have four-wheel drive," he said. "And a radio. We can listen to weather reports, but the three-day forecast is clear and cold." He turned to smile at her. "I checked the Weather Channel this morning before you woke up."

The cowboy's sense of direction was impressive. Not only did he drive the black Ranger out of a maze of airport roads, but he also located the interstate, muttering something about "88" and "90" and which one was better. He bought a handful of maps at a gas station, proceeded to a shopping center for dog food, sleeping bags, blankets, warm jackets and numerous other supplies designed for an emergency.

"You have to be prepared for the worst, sweetheart," he explained, shoving the bags of food into the back of the Ranger. Then he climbed behind the steering wheel and started the car. Doris, refusing the back seat, claimed a wool blanket tucked on the floor at Dylan's feet.

"The worst? What exactly would that be?" She had visions of freezing to death in the middle of South Dakota—or was it North Dakota that bordered Montana?

He leaned over as casually as if putting his arm around her was something he did every day. Will gave her a quick kiss that made her cold toes tingle, then released her to put on his seat belt. "Don't worry," the man said. "I've got everything figured out."

And by the time they reached the Holiday Inn outside of Davenport, Iowa, Dylan was very much convinced that he had spoken the truth.

"TWO ROOMS," DYLAN SAID, running up to the car. "One-oh-eight and one-ten."

"Where?"

"Around the back," she said, pointing to the corner of the three-story motel. "Follow me."

Will almost laughed. Follow her? What else would he rather do? He put the car in gear and kept a careful eye on Dylan as she hurried along the lighted sidewalk. The parking lot was half-empty, so he parked the car right in front of the doors to their rooms, which were conveniently side by side.

Doris hopped on the front seat and barked her excitement.

"Shh," he said. "You're not supposed to exist."

Here it was, almost six o'clock, and they were barely in Iowa. They'd stopped several times for Doris to relieve herself at recently plowed rest areas, had a quick lunch at a Burger King after leaving Doris snuggling into her blanket, and only took one wrong exit. They should have gotten closer to Des Moines, but Will didn't mind the pace. He wasn't about to risk driving at night, so as long as they arrived at the ranch by Christmas—and in one piece—that was all that mattered.

But spending each night with Dylan's luscious body tucked next to his in bed would be pretty damn good, too.

5

"WHAT'S THE BEST VACATION you've ever had?"

Will looked up from slicing a piece of meat from the slab of medium-rare tenderloin on his plate. The steakhouse adjoining the motel had lived up to its self-proclaimed Biggest Steaks in Iowa sign, which made a hungry man happy. The woman across the table from him might as well have been from another country. Despite the long day in the car, she looked as elegant and beautiful as if she'd just come from a fancy health spa. She reached for her wineglass and waited for an answer.

"Guess," he dared her, hoping to shake that ever-present composure.

"Camping. Mountain climbing. Cavorting with grizzly bears. Catching trout," she said. "Am I right?"

He shook his head. "Not even close."

She took a sip of wine and kept her gaze steady on his. "Hmm. Club Med? An exotic island adventure with a special lady?"

"Not yet, but I'm willing." He grinned. "Are you partial to beaches and hot sand?"

Dylan shrugged. "At times."

He suffered an immediate stab of jealousy. He blinked at the vision of Dylan topless on a hot beach while some dumb hunk with muscles the size of footballs rubbed oil on—

"I'm waiting," she said. "We might as well get to know each other, you know."

He could think of a few more interesting ways to do that besides talking about vacations, but Will behaved himself. "It would have to be a tie between a trip to Boston and the time the family went to Disney World when I was ten."

"Why Boston?" Her fingers stroked the stem of her wineglass and Will took a deep breath and looked away, to her mouth.

"I won a state debating contest in high school. The prize was getting to compete nationally, in Boston. It was the first time I'd seen a city that was so old." He smiled, remembering how excited he'd been when he'd seen Paul Revere's grave.

"How did you do?"

"I came in eighth. A ranch kid who'd been driving tractors since he was nine had to debate the value of raising the driving age to eighteen. Boston was a hell of a long way from the ranch."

"And Disney World? That must have been a long way from the ranch, too." She picked up a French fry with her fingers and took a bite.

"Yeah. The highlight of the trip was seeing an alligator," he announced, laughing at himself. "Jared saw it first, in a canal that was in the back of the campground. I was playing on a big pipe that hung out over the water, but Jared grabbed me before I fell in."

"You love your brother very much," Dylan said.

"What can I say—I'm a family man." He turned back to his dinner and picked up his steak knife once again.

"Yet you're not married."

He looked up and gave her a brief smile. "Nope. If and when I get married, it's gonna be for life." Will waited a second and then turned the question on her. "What about you?"

"The first time Mel and I went to London" was her prompt reply.

"I meant, have you ever been married?"

"Ah, no." Definitely looking nervous, she finished her wine and wiped her lips with a napkin.

"That didn't sound too convincing, sweetheart." He signaled the waitress for a refill on their wine.

"I was engaged once, a long time ago."

Will stopped chewing.

"He changed his mind," she explained.

"And broke your heart?" Now, this might explain the woman's independent streak.

"For a while. I got over it."

"Right."

She surprised him by laughing. "Don't look so serious or I won't tell you any more of my secrets. You've had your heart broken, too, I'm sure."

"Not really." He was grateful for the arrival of the waitress. She saved him from having to explain that he'd never been in love. He turned the conversation away from himself and asked what she and Melanie did in London.

Of course when the evening was over he kissed her in the hall in front of her door. Just a small kiss, a good-night gesture. Nothing to go crazy with lust over, though his body reacted as if Dylan had reached for his belt buckle instead of his arm.

So much for Iowa, Will decided, climbing into his bed with only Doris for company. The dog wasn't happy, either, but Will had had to put his foot down about where Doris would spend the night. If she had to go out, Will didn't want Dylan walking around in a dark parking lot.

And at least the dog kept his feet warm.

THEY SPENT Thursday driving from Iowa to Omaha, just west of the Nebraska border. Rain had slowed their progress, along with a late start. Will didn't mind stopping early when the rain turned to sleet and the visibility became poor. This time they were on the second floor of a Luxury Inn that allowed small dogs, and tonight they shared connecting rooms.

"So Doris can go back and forth," Will explained, dropping the key in Dylan's palm.

"Good idea."

Maybe, Will decided. Or not such a good idea, considering how easy it would be to open the door between them and make love to Dylan Briggs. He didn't think she'd slam the door in his face—at least not right away. He caught her looking at him sometimes, as if she couldn't figure him out. As if she liked looking at him, but didn't want to admit it.

It was still sleeting, so Will left his traveling companions in the motel and crossed the street to Pizza Hut. After placing his order, he went next door to a convenience store and bought beer, wine, a corkscrew, dog biscuits and a box of chocolate-covered doughnuts. By the time he returned to his room at the Luxury Inn—which actually was pretty nice—he was wet, frozen, hungry and glad to be inside.

"My hero," Dylan said, holding Doris back from the door. The dog seemed to recognize the smell of pizza and tried to jump up to sniff the box.

"Don't get too close," Will told Dylan. "I'm dripping." She reached into the bathroom and grabbed a towel.

"Here." She dropped the towel on his head and took the pizza box from him. "You know, this traveling life isn't too bad. What's in the bag?"

"Alcohol. Do you want beer or wine?" Will placed the bag on a round table in front of the picture window. Dylan had drawn the drapes and the room felt warm and private.

"Wine, please. I'll get the glasses." She disappeared into the bathroom again and came out with two glasses. Will draped his wet jacket over the back of a chair, tossed Doris a dog biscuit and opened the wine. He poured Dylan's wine, helped himself to a beer and ate four pieces of pizza before taking Doris and opening the door to his room.

"We'd be happy to stay with you," he told Dylan, who had followed them to the door.

"Take a hot shower," she said, ignoring the offer. "So you don't catch cold."

"I'm not going to catch cold."

He kissed her, something that was easily becoming a habit. He cradled her face in his hands and kissed her thoroughly, teasing her tongue with his own and feeling the heat rise between them. This time she moved closer to him, swept those elegant fingers along his sides, made a little sound of pleasure against his mouth. When he ended the kiss, it was with great reluctance, but he sensed she was a woman who wouldn't be rushed. She definitely was a woman who was not easily seduced.

"You know where I am," he told her. "If you need me."

"I appreciate that." Her smile almost made him kiss her again, but she stepped back before he reached for her. "I'll leave the door open a few inches," she said. "For Doris."

"Yeah. For Doris." He ran his hands through his hair and watched the door partially close. It opened again and Dylan handed him the rest of the beer.

"In case you get thirsty," she said.

So at the end of the day he was alone in a motel room, without even Doris to talk to. He opened a beer, turned on the television and checked the Weather Channel. Snow would be good. A blizzard would keep them in this hotel. The power would go off and they would need to stay warm by crawling into bed together.

He figured Dylan's body generated a lot of heat. He'd like to know what pleased her, where she liked to be touched, how she liked to be kissed. He thought of several places on that luscious body he could explore with his mouth and hands before he entered her. Beneath all that calm, cool, unruffled persona lay a woman who kissed as if she wondered what it would be like to touch him, too.

Or maybe that was only wishful thinking. Jared would laugh if he could see him now. "You've got it bad," his brother would say.

Yeah. He didn't know what he was going to do about Dylan Briggs once they reached the ranch. He couldn't picture waving goodbye and never seeing her again. Damn. He might be in love.

DYLAN DIDN'T THINK SHE should be having so much fun. Driving through the Midwest in December was risky; driving with a stranger through the Midwest in December was nothing short of insane.

Call her crazy, but she was having a good time. Melanie was not going to believe this. In fact, Dylan had deliberately not answered her cousin's telephone messages to tell her she was on her way. Let Mel think she was drinking rum out of a coconut on a Caribbean Princess cruise ship.

Twenty minutes west of Omaha lay an enormous antiques center, a huge warehouse-style building that even had its own billboard advertisement. She must have gasped, because Will slowed the car.

"What?"

She pointed to the warehouse, with Antiques in huge black letters above the doors. "My idea of heaven."

"We've only been on the road for fifteen minutes," he pointed out.

"There's a Cracker Barrel. You could eat breakfast while I shopped."

"I could, even though I polished off three of those chocolate doughnuts an hour ago while you were still in the shower," Will said. "Or I could keep driving to Montana. Do you know how *big* Nebraska is?"

"No. I don't have your fascination for maps." She smiled, noticing he was about to take the next exit, an access road that should lead them to the antiques "mall," gas station, restaurant and a couple of motels. "Too bad I didn't know this was here. I could have shopped last night." Shopping would have been better than lying awake half the night because Will was sleeping on the other side of the wall. Shopping was safer than lust and certainly less time-consuming.

"You're not going to find Paris-type antiques in Omaha," he warned, as if he shopped for collectibles for a living.

"I'll risk the disappointment." She tucked the blanket around a sleepy Doris as Will drove up in front of the metal building. "Give me an hour."

"Thirty minutes."

"Forty-five?"

He sighed. "Deal."

She leaned over and kissed him on the cheek before she hopped out of the car. "I owe you one."

"Never say that to a man who's seen you in a nightgown."

She felt her cheeks redden. "I meant—"

"Go," Will ordered. "But if you're not out of there in forty-five minutes I'm leaving without you."

She grabbed her purse and ran.

Many hours later, when they had made it as far as North Platte and were settled in one of the motels that lined Interstate 80 there, Will left Doris asleep in his room and drove Dylan to a steak house he'd seen from the highway.

"Look," he said, sipping a whiskey and water. "We've got to start moving along a little faster."

"How far did we go today?" She ordered a small filet and sipped a vodka martini. She felt like celebrating, having scored four quilts, one quilt top, four pairs of embroidered pillowcases and enough art deco kitchenware to make her clients in Arlington weep with joy. Will hadn't held her to the forty-five-minute time limit. He'd taken Doris for a long walk, then charmed the cashiers at the antique mall into letting him bring the little dog inside to wander the aisles with him. She could easily love a man like this.

"Not even three hundred and fifty miles." He frowned and looked around the dark restaurant. "I can't believe we only made it to North Platte."

"It's the home of Buffalo Bill," Dylan said. "There's even a gift shop that looks like a fort. Did you see it?"

"Yes. And don't even think about it."

"What happened to that charming cowboy—"

"Rancher."

"That charming *rancher*," she continued unperturbed, "who said 'Hey, I have a good idea, let's rent a car and drive to Montana'?"

"He was crazed with lust at the time."

"Was?" The revelation pleased her, which was silly. But still—

"Is. Was. Whatever." Will shrugged. "Don't worry about it."

"I'm not worried," she said, draining her martini.

"I gave up sex a year ago, so I don't worry about that kind of thing anymore."

His eyes were very dark as he stared at her. "What kind of thing?"

"Seduction. Sex. Should I or shouldn't I." After very bad dates with Prince Charming fakes, she'd decided to work more and play less. D.C. was full of handsome men who knew how to use their charm to get what they wanted, which meant a smart woman had to know bull when she heard it. And she heard a lot of it. "I got tired of all the games, so I gave it up. I still date, of course."

"Of course." He still wore that amazed look.

"But sex? Not worth the trouble."

"You must have been going out with the wrong men."

Yes, Dylan thought, looking at her rancher. She had no doubt that none of the men in her past could compare with the man across the table. She was halfway in love with him already, but she knew it couldn't last. They were too different, lived in two different worlds and—

"You gave up—" He paused as the waitress delivered their salads, then leaned across the table. "You gave up sex? Why?"

"It made life more simple." She took a bite of lettuce while Will stared at her as if he couldn't tell if she was joking or not. "This is delicious. Aren't you hungry?"

"Very." But he didn't pick up his fork immediately. Instead he waved at the waitress and motioned for seconds on drinks. "Haven't you ever wanted to change your mind?"

Oh, yes, she wanted to say. *Starting three nights ago in Chicago when a cowboy kissed me.*

"Dylan?"

She realized she hadn't answered the question. And the question made her huffy. "I don't think that's any of your business."

But instead of backing off, the rancher smiled. It was a very satisfied, very male smile, as if he knew damn well she'd thought about making love to a cowboy each and every night they'd been together.

"WHO GETS DORIS TONIGHT?"

"I do," Will replied, following her down the hall to their rooms. This time they were across the hall from each other.

Dylan stopped in front of his door. "You had her last night."

"Well, sure. Because I don't want her waking you up in the middle of the night to go out and then you going outside by yourself—"

"Will."

He stopped. "What?"

"Did she wake you to go out last night?"

"No." He had hoped she would, just so he could have an excuse to go out and get some air. He wasn't sleeping well lately. He dreamt of blue satin and white breasts and golden hair and legs that wrapped around—

"That's settled, then."

Will unlocked the door to his room and Dylan followed him inside, closing the door behind her. "Doris, come on, girl."

The dog greeted them as if they'd been gone for a week. Dylan knelt down and stroked her head and the dog wriggled in ecstasy. Will knew when he was defeated.

"Okay," he said. "You win. But I'll take her out first."

"Thank you." Her smile made his groin ache.

"I'll bring her to you in a little while. Don't open the door unless you know it's me."

When she left, he groaned. He'd walk the dog, take a cold shower and then knock on Dylan's motel room door. What was wrong with this picture?

Everything, it turned out. Because an hour later, when Dylan let him into her room, she wore that blue nightgown. But tonight she'd used her winter coat as a robe, giving her the appearance of a seductive bag lady. Her cell phone was pressed to her ear and she put her fingers to her lips to signal him to be quiet.

"I'll tell her, I promise," she said into the phone. "I will, Mom, don't worry."

Will unhooked the leash from Doris's collar and watched her leap onto one of the double beds. The covers were mussed, as if Dylan had already been in bed. The bed pillows were shoved against the headboard and, on the other side of a nightstand, Dylan's suitcase lay open on the other bed. He sat down next to the dog and tried not to see a pink silk thong tossed on top of a makeup bag. In fact, he deliberately turned away because he had no desire to take another cold shower.

"No," Dylan said. "It's going to be wonderful. We have all sorts of things planned. Western things."

Will looked at her. Western things?

She caught his eye and shrugged. "Yes, I love you, too. Bye." She turned the phone off and sat down on the bed across from him, her knees touching his. He noticed that she shut the suitcase lid.

"Too late," he said. "I saw them."

Dylan pretended she didn't know what he was talking about. "That was my mother."

"Is everything okay?" He thought it was strange that Dylan didn't want to spend Christmas with her family, but that wasn't his business any more than the pink thong was. Or the "I don't have sex" way of life.

"Everything's fine."

"I see you dressed up for me." He shifted his legs so his knees enclosed hers. He figured that was about as intimate as it was going to get, so he'd better enjoy it while it lasted.

Her chin lifted. "I was cold."

Will reached over and took her hands in his. Her fingers were cool, so he rubbed them with gentle motions. "Better?"

"Yes, but—"

"What?" He brought her hands to his lips and kissed each fingertip. It was a silly gesture, and from the look on her face he figured she wanted to laugh. "Go ahead."

"Hmm?"

"Laugh at me. I don't mind."

"Your lips tickle," she confessed, and she freed her hands from his. But only to hook them around the back of his neck. "If I kiss you good-night and then kick you out of my room, will you hate me in the morning?"

"Why should tomorrow be any different?" He tugged her forward, lifted her onto his lap. He would have called this progress if he hadn't heard the "I don't have sex" warning over dinner. But he knew damn well she'd been thinking about it. With him.

She didn't seem to mind being wrapped in his arms, her bottom against his thighs. He found her lips again and kissed her for long, aching minutes. She was sweet and hot and irresistible. And she still wore her winter coat.

"I love kissing you," he said, "but don't you want to take your coat off?"

"That's a little risky."

"Well, yeah." He grinned and kissed her ear. "That's the fun part."

"I'm not a big risk-taker," she confessed. Her fingers caressed the nape of his neck, and the erection strained the fabric of his jeans. "Aside from this trip."

"The past few days have been pretty damn unusual," he agreed, managing to slip her coat from her shoulders and down her arms, exposing that satin gown and lots of pale, smooth skin. "Take this, for instance."

"Take what?" She shocked him when she ran her hands along his chest.

"What are you doing?" His throat had gone dry and he hoped that when the time came to leave her room, he would be a gentleman and go without crying.

"I don't know."

"Well, I do." He lifted her off of him and set her on the bed. "You're up to no good, sweetheart. And I think you're trying to torture me before you kick me out of here." Will eyed her lips, full and swollen and ready for more kissing, but he didn't know how much more control he had left. This particular woman had gotten under his skin and he was damn afraid that when she walked out of his life—probably in a few days—he was going to hurt. Big time.

"You started it," she pointed out, scooting her bare feet under the covers as she looked at him and laughed.

He tossed her coat, still spread over his lap, to the floor and moved to face her. "I did not."

"It was that finger-kissing move. Do all your women like that?"

"Yeah," he said. "They stand in line for hours for the experience."

She laughed again, which should have killed his lust, but didn't. She had a sexy laugh, and the way she looked in bed, all that golden hair scrunched up against the pillows, was something he wouldn't mind seeing every night for the rest of his life.

Now, that was a scary thought, but worth pursuing...tomorrow. "You can't resist me," he said. "So if you're serious about this 'no sex' thing, tell me now."

Dylan sighed and her smile faded. "It would get too complicated, Will. I'm just not the type for casual, let's-have-fun-and-get-naked sexual encounters."

"And you think I am?" He moved one hand along the blanket and tweaked the lump that was her big toe.

"I don't know. I hope not, but—"

"You're playing it safe."

"Yes." She was one very cool lady, Will realized. And he noticed that her hand trembled when she reached up to push her hair behind her ear. She wasn't as unaffected by him as she pretended to be. A good sign, because he was afraid his hands might shake, too. This woman had become too important to him.

"I guess I'd better go," he said, but when he stood he leaned over and touched her lips with his. It should have been the kind of kiss that said "good night," but it quickly turned into an embrace that said something else much more passionate: "I want you."

He'd intended to leave her, to kiss her and leave her and go to his room. But that proved harder than he expected, because she rose up on her knees and looped her arms around his neck. His hands swept down her spine, smoothed the sweet curves of her waist and moved higher to caress satin-covered breasts. Her nipples beaded under his touch and she moaned against his mouth.

Will lifted his lips from hers a bare fraction. "Sweetheart, this might be a good time to tell me to leave."

"I'm going to regret this," Dylan muttered, but she rose up on her knees and reached for him.

"Not if I can help it," Will said, after one very long, very hot kiss that ended with his shirt unbuttoned and her nightgown falling off one shoulder. He figured his heart must be pumping about a hundred beats a minute, but somehow he managed to move a grumpy Doris to the other bed, turn off the light, take off the rest of his clothes and find the condoms he'd put in the new wallet he bought before leaving Chicago.

And then one very naked, very aroused rancher joined Dylan in the bed.

She lay on her side facing him, the slippery gown teasing his bare thighs as it brushed against him. "Could you do me one favor," she whispered, rubbing her palm along his chest.

"Anything." He moved closer, touched her earlobe with his nose and smelled the faint trace of vanilla shampoo. He ran his hand along her hip and lower, to bunch the fabric and lift it, higher and higher until she was exposed from the waist down.

"I'm out of practice."

"We'll take it slow," he murmured, assuming she'd be a little nervous.

"Fast would be better."

His hand stilled, his thumb in the crease of her thigh. "I'd kinda like to take my time." He moved his hand, his thumb finding a place that made her inhale with a sharp little sound. "Like this," he said, spreading her thighs open with his hand. He bent over her to kiss a path from her neck and lower, to the tip of one full breast. Nudging the material aside, his lips found her nipple and took it in his mouth.

"Will—"

He eased one finger inside of her and tugged on the peak of her breast at the same time. She was tight and ready for him and he thought he'd die from wanting to be inside of her, but he loved the touching, the way his fingers felt inside of her and the sounds she made when he brought her pleasure. He left her briefly, to reach for the condom, and then with a slow and deliberate motion guided himself into her. He rested his elbows on either side of her head and waited for her to open her eyes.

"Dylan," he whispered. "Sweetheart."

She lifted her hips, took him deeper, looked into his eyes and drew a ragged breath. "I like the way you take your time."

"Hang on," he said, moving deeper until he filled her. "The best is yet to come."

Her laugh was broken by another gasp when he slowly withdrew a few inches and then moved into her again, deep and sure. He found her mouth; she clung to his shoulders. He was kissing her when she came, her climax gripping him like a hot fist, urging him on to find his own release. When it came it was fast and hard, and he lifted his mouth from hers in order to let out a hoarse cry.

Long moments passed before Dylan spoke, but he could feel her heart beating under his chest.

"Wow," she said. "I've never had 'cowboy sex' before."

"*Rancher* sex," he corrected, barely able to breathe. "Oh, hell. Call it anything you want as long as we can do it again."

"We can. When?"

He tipped over onto his side, closed his eyes and listened to Doris snore from the other bed. "You have to give me a few minutes."

"I'm not going anywhere." Dylan's hand slid up

his thigh, caressed the exhausted part of his anatomy into perking up with renewed interest.

"Well," he said, his voice hoarse. "This is interesting."

"Mmm." She rolled onto her side and her breasts nudged his chest. "We don't have to get up early tomorrow, do we?"

"Sweetheart," he said, wanting nothing more than to bury himself inside her body again, "at this rate, we're never leaving Nebraska."

6

"ARE WE THERE YET?"

"Very funny."

Dylan smiled. This afternoon she would see Mel and the baby. The weather had cleared, tomorrow was Christmas Eve, and after they passed Billings, Will said the ranch was about a three-hour drive off the interstate.

It had been quite a trip. On Saturday morning they'd slept late, and with good reason, too. He woke her with kisses, so by the time she was awake she was also fully aroused, Will's mouth trailing down her abdomen, working magic between her thighs. He'd started slowly, teasing her with light flicks of his tongue. She quivered when his fingers opened her, cried out when his tongue found yet another place to brand her and relentlessly, effortlessly, surprisingly brought her to a mind-shattering climax. She hadn't been too sleepy to return the favor, though. She'd rather liked the power to make his breath catch when she'd held the hottest and hardest part of him in her hand. She'd bent over him, run her lips along his shaft. She'd teased him with her tongue before taking him in her mouth.

He'd cried out, but she didn't stop exploring and tasting and learning what brought him pleasure. And when he grit his teeth and lifted her from him, he'd tipped her over on her back and entered her with a fierceness that was part passion and part possession.

And now, remembering, Dylan unbuttoned her coat and turned down the heat inside the SUV. Will caught her gaze and winked at her. Which meant he was remembering, too.

She was terribly afraid she was falling in love with him. What else could explain her physical reaction to this man?

They managed to drive two hundred miles to Cheyenne, Wyoming, on Saturday before lust overtook them at the sight of a Holiday Inn. That night, long after they'd made love, Will slid out of bed and apologized for leaving her.

"I need to call home," he said, kissing her one more time before he tucked the covers over her bare shoulders. He took the phone into the bathroom and shut the door; she heard him laughing while Dylan had snuggled with Doris and gone to sleep.

On Sunday she'd awakened wrapped in his arms, her breasts against his chest.

"I love waking up with you," he'd said. And then he'd proved it. The man knew exactly how to make her body turn to jelly in ten seconds.

Much later, when they were packing to leave, she remembered to ask him about the phone call. "Is everything okay?"

"Yeah." He'd grinned. "Couldn't be better. I didn't tell Jared that you were coming, too," he said. "I thought you'd want to surprise Melanie."

"Thank you." She resisted the urge to tug him back into their rumpled bed, so on Sunday they'd traveled farther, to Sheridan, because Will said if they didn't get in six hours of driving time he'd have to get her up at dawn the next day in order to make up the time.

An idle threat, Dylan assumed, because there was no doubt that neither one of them liked getting out of bed. She was in love, of course. She caught herself smiling for no reason, inhaling the scent of his pillow while he was in the shower, talking baby-talk to Doris and turning into a fluttering mess every time the man looked at her as if he couldn't wait to get to a motel. Yes, she assured herself, she was in love, maybe for the first time in her entire self-sufficient life. She'd fallen so hard she even had fantasies about the man's hands. She couldn't wait to see Mel and tell her all about it.

"Can we stop here, in Billings?"

"Is it important?"

"I want to buy a toy for Beth." She'd brought presents for Mel and the baby, little packages that she could tuck in her suitcase, but she wanted to make the holiday festive for the baby's first Christmas. She wanted to buy toys and a little red velvet holiday dress and maybe even socks with Santa Claus faces imprinted on them.

He followed signs to the Rimrock Mall, which looked huge, and found a parking spot near the Herberger's entrance. "I guess I'll run in and get a bow for Doris. I sure as hell hope my mother likes her."

"Why wouldn't she?" Dylan leaned down and gave the dog's head a pat.

Will shut off the ignition. "Because my dad—he died eight years ago—gave my mother a collie pup when she was sixteen. I thought Doris might cheer her up, but the more I'm with her, the more I realize that this dog looks nothing like a collie."

"Yes, she does. A little, anyway," Dylan assured him. "She's just a lot smaller. Your mother will love her." Doris licked her hand. "You be a good girl. I'll be back in forty minutes."

And she was, after a quick trip to K-B Toys, JCPenney and two other stores. Her bags were awkward, but she was full of Christmas spirit when she approached the Ranger and saw Will walking the dog, a bright red bow tied to her collar, toward her.

"Doris," Dylan called. "You look so beautiful!"

"I felt like an idiot," Will said, gesturing toward the bow. "But the salesgirl insisted."

"You took Doris into the mall?"

"Sure. Nobody seemed to care and she minded her manners. What the hell is all this stuff?" Will opened the passenger door and, after unhooking Doris from the leash, lifted her back to her bed on the floor.

"Presents. Lots of presents. Of course Mel won't fly, so we'll have to take the train home. But we'll ship everything we can't carry and to heck with the cost." She walked around to the back of the SUV, opened the door and started to unload the packages. Will stepped closer.

"What if Melanie doesn't want to go home?"

"What are you talking about?"

They were in business together. They were best friends, closer than sisters.

"I think there's something you should know," he said, leaning against the car. His breath made little puffs of white smoke when he talked. "My brother is in love with Melanie. He thinks she might feel the same way about him, too, so if it's mutual—" He stopped and grinned down at her. "Pretty cool matchmaking on my part, huh?"

"*If* it's mutual," she repeated. "That's a pretty big 'if.'"

"Uncle Joe said he'd bet money on it."

"How nice. So *if* Melanie is in love with Jared, then what?"

"She'll be staying on, at Graystone, of course."

"Just like that."

"Sure. Why not?" His satisfied smile faded.

"Why *not?*" Dylan couldn't believe the question.

"Because she has a job, a business she helps me run. Her life is in Washington, not Montana."

"So?" The man was clearly baffled. "She can't move?"

"She can't stay here. No one turns their whole life around after a few days with a cowboy, especially not Melanie."

"No one, huh?" He wasn't smiling now. In fact, he looked really hurt.

"I didn't mean it like that," she said, but she realized she wasn't sure if she did or not.

"Yeah. I get it. You were enjoying a road trip, entertaining yourself with cowboy sex for as long as it got you where you wanted to go, but it's not like it's anything more than a few days of fun. Is that how it went?"

"No." Suddenly it was very hard to breathe. She shut the double doors but stayed where she was. "You make it sound as if I deliberately seduced you, just to get a ride to Montana. I'm the one with the credit card and the driver's license, remember? You'd still be in Chicago if it wasn't for me."

"Could you get into the truck now? I'd like to get home today, not that I'd expect you to understand."

She followed him to the driver's side and watched as he opened the door. "And what's that supposed to mean?"

"I don't see you knocking over fences to get to your own family for Christmas. You have parents. Why aren't you with them instead of sticking your nose where it doesn't belong?"

She stood there, stunned and cold and hurt. "My parents are—never mind," she said, her voice so low she wondered if he could hear her over the wind that swept over the parking lot. "Maybe you're the one who doesn't understand anything."

He turned his back and climbed in, leaving Dylan no choice but to go around to the other side of the car. The door was already open, and when Dylan stepped inside, she realized that something was wrong.

Doris was gone.

WILL COULD HAVE KICKED himself all the way to the Canadian border for not shutting the car door after he'd put Doris inside. He'd been proud of his match-making and itching to share the fact that Jared and Melanie had hit it off—or at least Jared thought they had. He'd thought Dylan would be pleased, but nope. She couldn't imagine life with a cowboy.

Well, that put *him* in his place, all right. And here he'd been thinking of nothing else but making a future and keeping Dylan in his life. He'd fallen in love—and fallen hard, too. He thought he'd found the woman who was perfect for him in every way.

Well, a fool's born every minute, Uncle Joe would say.

And now this fool had lost his dog. His *mother's* dog. And his temper, too.

"Doris!" he'd called throughout the parking lot until his throat grew sore. He'd looked under cars, around corners and by the trash cans near the closest mall entrance. Dylan had done the same and had gone inside the mall to see if anyone had turned in a little brown-and-white dog with a red bow on its collar to the lost-and-found department. She'd been gone a long time when he saw her in front of the mall. She was handing out leaflets, and when Will jogged over to her, he could see the papers were actually flyers about Doris. There was a clever drawing of the dog with a bow around her neck and a Help Doris Come Home for Christmas headline above it. A phone number and promise of a reward were beneath the drawing.

"You did this?" He looked over her shoulder.

"I was an art major before I abandoned my family, set off across country and had sex with a cowboy." She didn't look at him.

"A simple 'yes' would do." Dylan ignored him, which was fine because she damn well wasn't his kind of woman to begin with. He'd been blinded by lust and her ability to rent a car.

Instead she handed a flyer to a mother leaving the mall with three young children. "If you see this dog, will you call me? Thanks!"

"It's been almost two hours," Will pointed out. "You can't stand here in the cold all afternoon."

"She has to be somewhere close," Dylan said,

sounding as if she was going to cry. "I'll bet she got out of the car to go to the bathroom."

"Or she smelled food. Maybe somebody saw her wandering around the parking lot and picked her up." Unless she had run out into the road and gotten hit, which made him feel sick to his stomach. Growing up with animals had made him accept death as part of ranch life, but he'd never gotten used to it. And he'd grown fond of the little dog he'd meant to bring home. Will cleared his throat. "I think I'll drive around the mall, check behind the mounds of snow."

"I'll stay here." She didn't look at him. Instead Dylan watched the parking lot as if Doris would appear any minute. Which she might, but Will was losing hope fast. It was pretty damn cold with the wind coming up as hard as it was. Doris could freeze to death.

It was growing dark when he broached the subject of leaving town.

"No," Dylan said, holding back tears. "Not without Doris."

"It's almost four o'clock. We can't stay here all night." The look on her face told him she expected to do just that.

"I'm not leaving her. She's your mother's Christmas gift and she must be so scared and wondering where we are. She probably thinks we deserted her."

"She's only known us a few days," he pointed out, yet he was surprised by Dylan's refusal to leave.

"That doesn't matter," Dylan said. "She *loves* us."

"Yeah? Even after only a few days?" The look he gave her made her swallow hard.

"A woman at the Hallmark store told me about the Billings Animal Shelter," she said. "I called and got directions. They're open until six and they hold strays for seventy-two hours. You never know. Someone might bring her in."

"You want to go there and wait?"

"Every store in the mall has my cell phone number. They'll call if anyone finds her. I've called every veterinarian's office to see if an injured dog was brought in. They have my number, too."

"Then let's go to the shelter. At least we can get warm." He almost put his arm around her slumped shoulders, but thought better of it. Maybe it was better this way, breaking up before they'd even begun. Maybe—probably—it wouldn't have worked out, anyway.

DYLAN WALKED PAST THE DOGS in their cages as most of them—big and small—barked at her. Not vicious barking, but she could almost here them saying, "Hi, hi! Pick me! Take me home!"

It was enough to break her heart, if it had been in one piece to begin with. Between losing Doris and facing Will's anger, she felt awfully battered. But she forced herself to look in each cage, hoping to find Doris wagging her tail in greeting. At the end of the cement aisle a tiny, golden-haired dog curled up in a circle looked at Dylan out of calm brown eyes.

"Hi," she said, stooping down to see him—or her.

"That's Ben," the shelter volunteer said. "He's some kind of Pekingese mix, we think, from his flat face and all that hair. He's one of our seniors. Neutered, with most of his teeth and in pretty good health. His elderly owner died and the kids didn't want him, so here he is."

"That's so sad." Dylan started to cry. "Sorry," she said, reaching for her purse. "It's been a terrible day."

"Maybe you'll find your dog tonight. Or tomorrow," the woman said, but she didn't sound hopeful. "You never know."

"That's true," Dylan said. "Can I pet Ben?"

"Sure." She unlatched the cage, which allowed Dylan to reach in and scratch Ben's ears, which he seemed to like a lot. He didn't stand up right away, but eventually crept closer to sniff her knees. "You don't smell very good, Ben, do you know that?"

"Dylan?" She turned to see Will standing in the aisle.

"What?"

"How about getting something to eat?"

"No, thanks." She continued to pet Ben, who now rested his chin on her knee. She'd rather eat canned dog food.

"Look," he said. "Maybe we could—"

Whatever he was going to say ended when her cell

phone rang. Dylan grabbed it out of her opened purse and clicked it on. *Please, please, please.* "Hello?" And then she listened to the words she longed to hear: *Are you the person missing a dog?*

SOMEONE WAS IN THE DOGHOUSE. And Will Stone knew exactly who that was, because he sat alone on the edge of his bed in a Billings motel while Dylan, the city woman he'd thought was so cold-hearted that she didn't bother to spend the holidays with her parents or think her cousin should fall in love with a Montana man or even that she herself would consider falling for a rancher, snuggled with two formerly abandoned mutts named Doris and Ben—both of whom she'd refused to leave Billings without.

So, this was one of those rare occasions when he was wrong about something. How about that.

Will opened the bottle of beer he'd bought at the bar downstairs and turned on the television, looking for the Monday night football game, but lost interest ten minutes later. He wanted to be with Dylan, but he'd be damned if he could think how to tell her he loved her without making a damn fool of himself.

It was going to be a long and lonely night.

ON THE MORNING of Christmas Eve, Dylan still had no idea what she was going to do. She couldn't spend Christmas at the Stones' ranch—she had not been invited, after all—so she would have to take the Ranger and find the nearest motel, even if she doubted there would be any such thing within fifty miles. And she would leave without Mel and Beth, she supposed, because Dylan pictured the ranch looking something like the Ponderosa, from the old TV show *Bonanza* that was on cable late at night. Mel wouldn't want to leave the comfort of the Ponderosa on Christmas Eve, especially if she had fallen in love with Will's older brother.

Will had taken her by surprise with that information. She pictured Mel still quiet and grieving, which wasn't at all the way she wanted her cousin to live. But did she have to fall in love with someone who lived so far away? And the truth was her feelings were still a little hurt because Mel had taken off to spend the holiday with strangers instead of her own family.

She'd shed a few tears over that one.

So on the morning of the twenty-fourth, when the cowboy knocked on her door, she was packed and ready. The two dogs had already been walked and Dylan wore her warmest sweater and two pairs of socks.

"Ready?" was all he said. He didn't look as if he'd slept much. Frown lines etched the corners of his mouth and his eyes were dark.

"Yes."

They made a quick run through the McDonald's drive-up window for breakfast and coffee before heading north on 87. A long time passed before Will spoke again. "Sleep well?"

"Not really." Why lie?

"The dogs keep you up?"

"No. They decided that Doris would sleep by my shoulders and Ben would keep my feet warm." She crushed her empty coffee cup and put it in the empty food bag.

"I didn't get to thank you for finding her."

"I didn't." She stared out the window at the gray sky and snow-covered plains. She even saw distant mountains, but they looked very far away. She wondered why Will was trying to be nice.

"But the kids' mother saw the flyer you made and figured out what had happened."

"I'm just glad Doris was okay." Twin nine-year-old girls had found the little dog in the parking lot—close to where the Ranger was parked—and had smuggled her home. The divorced parents—each of whom thought the other had lost their mind and bought a dog for the girls for Christmas—finally realized that the twins had picked up someone's lost pet. "For your mother's sake, too."

Another long period of silence followed. Doris snored softly at Dylan's feet and Ben, having claimed her lap, snuggled against her as close as he could get. He'd tolerated his bath last night and she'd had to use three little bottles of hotel shampoo in order to rid him of his kennel odor.

"Dylan."

"What?" He kept looking.

"Can we start over again, pretend we just met?"

"What do you mean?" She glanced toward him, but he gave her a brief smile before turning his attention back to the road.

"Well, say I saw you at some party in Washington. I could introduce myself. You'd tell me your name, we'd look each other over, like what we see, and sample some of those puffy shrimp things the waiter keeps hauling around."

"And then?" she asked, wondering where he was going with this.

"I'd ask what kind of work you did and you'd tell me you decorated things."

"I'm an interior designer," she said. "I have a shop in Georgetown called Dylan Designs."

"I'd act real impressed, of course," he said.

"Of course." She felt the ache around her heart easing.

"And you'd ask what I did. Which, by the way, you've never asked before."

"I thought you were a rancher."

"I am," Will said, glancing toward her again. "And at the party I'd tell you I'm from Montana and I'm a lobbyist with a crop protection agency."

"And I'd say, 'Do you spend a lot of time in Washington?'"

"More and more. I think it's going to end up being

about six or eight months out of the year. My brother runs things at home. He's not much for the city. Then I'd say, 'Do you want another drink?'"

Dylan decided to play along. "No. I have to leave early. I've got an auction to go to in the morning."

"Then I'd get your phone number."

"But would you call?"

"The next day. I'd ask you out to dinner and you'd say yes." He smiled at her then, which caused that familiar weakness in her bones. "One thing would lead to another and—"

"And?"

"You'd forget that 'no sex' thing you had going and pretty soon we'd be spending a lot of nights together."

"Sounds like fun." She could almost picture it. If she'd met him at a party he would have charmed her into another date. And another.

"More than fun," he said, his voice more serious now. He didn't say anything for a few minutes. Instead he concentrated on driving, slowing the car to pull into a "scenic view" area on the side of the road. He stopped the car and turned to her, hooking his arm over the steering wheel.

"More than fun," he repeated, looking at her with an intense expression on his handsome face. "I'd start thinking that you were the woman I wanted to spend the rest of my life with. I'd be thinking about marriage and kids and..." His gaze dropped to Ben and then lifted to Dylan again. "Dogs. I'd wonder if you and I could make a life together."

Dylan took a deep breath. "And if I couldn't see myself giving up my business and spending the rest of my life on a ranch?"

"I don't believe that was part of the deal. I figured two smart people who loved each other could come up with a compromise."

"Such as?"

He shrugged. "Living in D.C. when Congress is in session. Holidays and summers in Montana. Nothing is impossible, sweetheart."

Dylan didn't say anything for a long moment. She pet Ben's soft head and listened to Doris's heaving breathing and tried to imagine the scenario that Will had just outlined. "And if I—if I agreed with you, then what happens?"

"I'd tell you I love you."

"I'd tell you that I love you, too."

Will unfastened his seat belt and leaned across the seat, his arm enclosing her shoulders. And he smiled. "Then I'd ask you to come home with me for Christmas. To meet the family, including my eccentric aunt Bitty and my wise old uncle Joe. My mother and brother will be real happy for us."

"My parents would be, too, though they're celebrating their thirtieth wedding anniversary this week. On a cruise. They asked me to go, but I didn't think they needed company on their dream vacation."

"No," he said, his mouth hovering close to hers. He brushed his lips across hers, once, twice, before speaking. "Of course not."

"So you'd be free for Christmas?"

"Yes," Dylan said, reaching for him. "I would. But I'd planned to spend the holidays with my cousin."

"Bring her along."

"She'd like that."

This time the kiss lasted a very long, breathtaking time. When Will finally lifted his head, he didn't go far. "And on Christmas Eve—today *is* Christmas Eve, right?" She nodded. "I'd ask you to marry me."

Dylan blinked back tears. "You would?"

"Yeah." He waited, his eyes uncertain.

"I'd say yes," she managed to whisper.

"For better or worse, in sickness and in health, with kids, dogs, road trips and lots of hot sex?"

"Absolutely. Forever and ever."

It was a long time before they spoke again.

"Well," he said, holding her close against him while Ben growled. "I guess we'd better get going. It's either that or get naked and crawl into the back seat."

She couldn't help laughing. "You are one romantic rancher."

"Yes, ma'am. I try."

Dylan smoothed her palms along the sharp planes of his face. She would be content to love this man for the rest of her life. "Start the car, cowboy. We don't want to miss Christmas."

_____Epilogue_____

"WELL, WHAT DO YOU THINK? Will she do?" Bitty stood next to Jenna and eyed the four young people gathered on the floor by the Christmas tree.

"She's perfect," Jenna replied, turning to beam at the little brown-and-white dog who sat on the couch as if she owned the place already. "I can't believe Will found her and went to all that trouble to bring her home to me for Christmas."

"You're talking about the dog," Bitty said, exasperated. "I'm talking about the girl."

"Dylan?" She led her aunt over to the sofa and helped her get settled. "She's a lovely young woman and I think she and Will look happy. He told me he's going to make it official as soon as they pick out an engagement ring." The arrival of Melanie's cousin had been quite a surprise, and it had taken another hour to sort out Melanie's happy tears and Jared's proud expression. They'd announced their plans to marry in front of everyone over lunch.

And then Will made his own wedding announcement while Dylan blushed. Melanie was the first one to hug her. The baby cried, the dogs barked and Uncle Joe broke out a bottle of the best whiskey he could find in the liquor cabinet. Even the FedEx man, delivering the package from O'Hare with Will's wallet, had stayed to toast the happy couples and warm himself in front of the fireplace.

"Both boys getting married," Aunt Bitty said, reaching to lift Fluffy on her lap. The little Maltese wasn't accustomed to other dogs running around the house; she had spent the last twenty-four hours hiding behind Bitty's legs whenever Ben or Doris tried to make friends with her. "Isn't that something to think about. Grandchildren, Jenna. You're going to have lots of them."

"I hope so. I love the one I already have." Jenna watched Dylan take the baby from Melanie so she could open another gift.

"Come to Auntie Dylan," she said, kissing the baby's fat cheek. So the sophisticated designer who'd given thick bars of lavender-scented French soap to Aunt Bitty and her future mother-in-law liked babies as well as dogs.

It was difficult for Jenna to decide which Christmas gift she liked the most: Melanie, Doris, Dylan or Beth. All of a sudden there were three more females in the house and Jenna didn't feel quite so overwhelmed with men. She sat down on the couch and the little dog rested her head on Jenna's thigh and sighed with contentment.

Joe crossed the room and sat down in the chair

closest to Jenna. He put his new poker set on the coffee table. "Ain't that grand?"

"Yes, it certainly is. Jared said he found it in that secondhand store in Duggan. I guess Melanie dragged him in there." She smiled at her uncle and reached over to take his gnarled hand in hers. He gave it a squeeze.

"The boys' father would have been real proud."

Jenna, too choked with sudden tears to speak, rested her free hand on the dog's head for comfort. She smiled at her uncle and then heard Will calling her.

"Hey, Mom!"

She looked up to see her younger son lift Dylan's yellow dog from under the tree. For some reason Ben kept crawling in there to take a nap. "What, honey?"

"Didn't you bake any cookies this year?"

"They're under my bed," she replied, much to the amusement of her family. "You can bring one of the boxes down.

"Only one box? What about the rest of them?"

"I'm saving them," she answered, stroking her dog's ears.

"For what?"

Jenna smiled, knowing her boys would be the most handsome grooms in Montana. "For your wedding, of course."

There's something for everyone...

Behind the
Red Doors

From favorite authors

Vicki Lewis Thompson

Stephanie Bond

Leslie Kelly

A fun and sexy collection about the romantic encounters
that take place at The Red Doors lingerie shop.

Behind the Red Doors—
you'll never guess which one leads to love...

Look for it in January 2003.

HARLEQUIN®
Makes any time special ®

Visit us at www.eHarlequin.com

PHBTRD

$ **Saving Money** $
Has Never Been
This Easy!

Just fill out and send in this form from any October, November and December 2002 books and we will send you a coupon booklet worth a total savings of $20.00 off future purchases of Harlequin and Silhouette books in 2003.

Yes! It's that easy!

I accept your incredible offer!
Please send me a coupon booklet:

Name (PLEASE PRINT)

Address   Apt. #

City   State/Prov.   Zip/Postal Code

In a typical month, how many
Harlequin and Silhouette novels do you read?

❏ **0-2**   ❏ **3+**

097KJKDNC7   097KJKDNDP

Please send this form to:
In the U.S.: Harlequin Books, P.O. Box 9071, Buffalo, NY 14269-9071
In Canada: Harlequin Books, P.O. Box 609, Fort Erie, Ontario L2A 5X3

Allow 4-6 weeks for delivery. Limit one coupon booklet per household. Must be postmarked no later than January 15, 2003.

HARLEQUIN®
Makes any time special®

Silhouette®
Where love comes alive™

© 2002 Harlequin Enterprises Limited

If you enjoyed what you just read,
then we've got an offer you can't resist!

Take 2 bestselling love stories FREE!

Plus get a FREE surprise gift!

///////////////////////////////////////

Clip this page and mail it to Harlequin Reader Service®

IN U.S.A.	IN CANADA
3010 Walden Ave.	P.O. Box 609
P.O. Box 1867	Fort Erie, Ontario
Buffalo, N.Y. 14240-1867	L2A 5X3

YES! Please send me 2 free Harlequin Temptation® novels and my free surprise gift. After receiving them, if I don't wish to receive anymore, I can return the shipping statement marked cancel. If I don't cancel, I will receive 4 brand-new novels each month, before they're available in stores. In the U.S.A., bill me at the bargain price of $3.57 plus 25¢ shipping and handling per book and applicable sales tax, if any*. In Canada, bill me at the bargain price of $4.24 plus 25¢ shipping and handling per book and applicable taxes**. That's the complete price and a savings of 10% off the cover prices—what a great deal! I understand that accepting the 2 free books and gift places me under no obligation ever to buy any books. I can always return a shipment and cancel at any time. Even if I never buy another book from Harlequin, the 2 free books and gift are mine to keep forever.

142 HDN DNT5
342 HDN DNT6

Name	(PLEASE PRINT)	
Address	Apt.#	
City	State/Prov.	Zip/Postal Code

* Terms and prices subject to change without notice. Sales tax applicable in N.Y.
** Canadian residents will be charged applicable provincial taxes and GST.
  All orders subject to approval. Offer limited to one per household and not valid to current Harlequin Temptation® subscribers.
  ® are registered trademarks of Harlequin Enterprises Limited.

TEMP02   ©1998 Harlequin Enterprises Limited

Visit eHarlequin.com to discover your one-stop shop for romance:

buy books

♥ Choose from an extensive selection of Harlequin, Silhouette, MIRA and Steeple Hill books.

♥ Enjoy top Harlequin authors and *New York Times* bestselling authors in Other Romances: Nora Roberts, Jayne Ann Krentz, Danielle Steel and more!

♥ Check out our deal-of-the-week specially discounted books at up to 30% off!

♥ Save in our Bargain Outlet: hard-to-find books at great prices! Get 35% off your favorite books!

♥ Take advantage of our low-cost flat-rate shipping on all the books you want.

♥ Learn how to get FREE Internet-exclusive books.

♥ In our Authors area find the currently available titles of all the best writers.

♥ Get a sneak peek at the great reads for the next three months.

♥ Post your personal book recommendation online!

♥ Keep up with all your favorite miniseries.

HARLEQUIN®

Makes any time special®—online...

Visit us at
www.eHarlequin.com

HINTBB